I0619758

MURDER EVERY MAGGOT

Bronco Hammer

Sierra West Books

BOOKS BY BRONCO HAMMER

SoCal Noir Books by Bronco Hammer
Hollywood Scum Must Pay
Spank Me
JCPI
Pimps Must Die
Die You Commie Bastards
See You in Hell
Die You Filthy Animal
Man of Violence
I Stomp on your Throat
Dead Guy in the Alley, A Love Story
June Gloom
Murder every Maggot

Friendship Foundation Books by Bronco Hammer
Die You Slimy Maggot
Deep State Deadly

Other books by Bronco Hammer
Assholes from Space
Narc in the Dark

ACKNOWLEDGE-MENTS

Every reader is appreciated. I wish I could acknowledge all of you here but so many of you are wanted by the law or operate under an assumed identity that it is impossible to honor your names without risking a wave of unimaginable death and destruction to innocent civilians across the land.

I do need to mention the following people who provide advice and guidance throughout the book series. I seldom use their advice but they are fun to listen to. So, any errors which might appear in this literary masterpiece are my fault and not the fault of these few, we happy few, we band of readers. *(Thanks, Bill Shakespeare, for that chunk of inspiring inspiration).*

So, without further ado, here are just a few of the brain trust behind the greatness. I apologize for anyone I left off this list. Below are some the people who inspire and assist me in being the most dangerous writer in the world.

Jeff Trapp - Unnecessary violence consultant and contributor of an important line

Tim Fife - Cover model for Joe Tucker, senior consultant on matters of manliness

John Rolfe - Cover model for Johnny Dedd, SWAT advisor, and fast food consultant

Carlo DeBlasio - Shooting and blasting advisor

William Tullock - Character development advisor

John Cocchiola - He didn't do anything but I spelled his name wrong in the last book. Sorry.

Elvis Bray - American legend.

Holli Lawton - Grammar guru and Schrödinger's cat spotter.

Mike Ratke - Hired muscle and content advisor

Randy Lewis - Director of martial arts and motor jokes... but not really the martial arts part.

"A hero is someone who understands the responsibility that comes with his freedom." — Bob Dylan

"It is easier to find men who will volunteer to die, than to find those who are willing to endure pain with patience."
— *Julius Caesar*

"Audiences like to see the bad guys get their comeuppance" - *Charles Bronson*

Author's note

Joe Tucker previously appeared in 'Dead Guy in the Alley—A Love Story'

Johnny Deddario previously appeared in 'I Stomp on Your Throat' and 'Dead Guy in the Alley—A love Story'

Joan Vance Previously appeared in 'Dead Guy in the Alley—A love Story'

Mister Stump previously appeared in 'Dead Guy in the Alley—A love Story'

Cat previously appeared as other characters in Dead Guy in the alley - A love Story and June Gloom

One other favorite Bronco Hammer book character will also make a brief cameo in which he will kill some guys, make out with a hot chick, and leave.

Unfortunately, all the bad guys from these Above mentioned books are deceased.

PRE-READ BRIEFING

Welcome aboard, find a seat and we'll start the briefing. In this book I'll be taking us back to Los Angeles, California. We'll revisit the characters from I Stomp on your Throat and Dead Guy in the Alley.

Obviously since Johnny Dedd is in this story, things will get violent for almost no reason at all. His cousin, Joe Tucker, is still kind of a puss, but he is also a guy who gets the job done.

I wrote this based on inspiration provided by the readers. I really enjoy having my readers be the cover models, providing story ideas, offering character suggestions, and having fun being part of the book projects. The books wouldn't happen without your input and support, so I thank you all so much.

You will need a bullet-resistant vest and a helmet to read this one... and probably a cocktail, so suit up and prepare to read.

Your pal,

Bronco Hammer - The most dangerous writer in

the world.

PREFACE

Offices of the Los Angeles County Organized Crime Task Force

The conference room was too large for three people. It made everyone seem smaller than they were. The acoustic ceiling and drab pre-fab walls left the voices flattened and tinny in spite of the rising tempers.

"I don't care about this mistaken notion of pervasive political corruption which you seemingly refuse leave alone, Detective Vance. Government corruption cases are FBI matters and you were never assigned that kind of case to begin with. You have no hard evidence to support your theory and the idea that a high ranking political figure could undermine the police department is patently ridiculous. Stay off of it and go to Long Beach. Watch the Yakuza guys like the Captain just ordered you to. The Bureau can handle your corruption information... send it to them." The chubby law enforcement executive was near breathless as he gasped out a self-righteous but feeble ass chewing. His doughy face was flushed and sweaty. His words delivered all the force of a mildly foul smell.

"We can't give it to the Bureau..." Vance explained. "We believe the US Attorney may be part of the conspiracy. We've identified potential ties to organized crime."

The headache inducing government florescent bulbs in the ceiling added to Vance's pounding headache and sense of being trapped in the waiting room for entering Hades.

The LAPD Deputy Chief's fleshy round face reddened even more. His boiling rage pinched his cheeks and eyebrows together causing his normal 'sleepy dog' squint to be even more pronounced than usual. "I've had about enough of your preposterous conspiracy theories, Detective... the US Attorney is a close friend of mine. And your massive corruption pipe dream is not a task force case. In fact, it's borderline insubordination and maybe even malfeasance. Dammit, we have FBI agents on this team. How disrespectful can you be? They are professionals. Do you want to get sent back to Beverly Hills PD? I don't know why you were ever assigned to the task force anyway unless your Chief just wanted to get rid of you."

As the Deputy Chief ended his rambling rant he appeared as though he was on the verge of a stroke. Vance knew she needed to shut up and follow orders but her sense of duty overwhelmed her sense of career survival.

"But Chief..."

The Captain interrupted, probably saving her from an immediate suspension. "I think you've wasted enough of the Chief Gray's time, Detective Vance. You have your orders. You and your partner need to hit the street now if you are going to be at the harbor before the exchange and make the arrest on the Yakuza deal. It will go down between four and six this morning. Stay on channel Tac-14... I'll be monitoring. I want this done right."

Vance responded with a half-hearted, "Yes sir." This argument wasn't a hill to die on, at least not right now.

In the hallway, her partner Detective Tommy Chang, waited. He wasn't happy about getting dragged in again. He wore the face of a man waiting to see the proctologist." How did it go, Vance? Did they listen?"

"How did it go? Well, we didn't get fired yet... But the night is still young."

"That bad?"

"Yeah. That bad."

Two hours later, Tommy was dead.

CHAPTER 1

Joe Tucker's Bedroom - Los Angeles, California

Sure, I'll join you for a drink. I love the grass skirt, by the way... very stylish. And the whole topless thing really works for you... What's that? Would I care for a massage, as well? Why, certainly, how could I refuse such a generous offer?

Such a pleasant dream... but the unwelcome pressure on my chest interrupted the slumber fantasy. My supermodel, mai tai, and tiki bar vanished and I was rudely shoved into reality.

I stirred sufficiently awake to discover two yellow unblinking eyes inches from the tip of my nose.

How did my neighbor's black cat get inside my apartment again? Why was it on my bed? What makes it think it is okay to stand on my chest and stare at me?

I looked around. My Colt Diamondback was out of reach... In fact, I wasn't sure where it I left it. My best guess is, it is somewhere among those clothes I see scattered imprecisely on the floor. What kind of loser misplaces his weapon... or tosses his clothes on the ground like some street drunk who decides to go the full monte just because he can?

Oh... me... I'm that loser... but I want to finish my dream.

I endeavored to slip back into my hangover-escaping slumber... maybe that girl was still at the tiki bar...on the seashore... in the warm breeze...

No joy.

The cat begins making kitty biscuits in my chest, claws piercing the sheet and digging into my skin deep enough to hurt.

My phone rings...

I can't see it.

Maybe it's because I have the pillow on my face. Or did I go blind? No, I just saw the cat.

Where's my phone?

Probably somewhere in that pile of wadded up clothes with the gun.

Shittiest morning ever.

This time of year in Southern California, one might as well be living in Alaska. It's dark most of the time. The sun comes up at seven and is down by a little after five. I can never guess the time between all the coastal marine layer, fog, smog, and dust in the air hiding what little daylight we have. But at least happy hour stays on schedule and the bars close at the same time as always giving me some frame of reference for these lost days of California winter. Christmas is coming... bah... humbug.

I fought to get up from the wadded-up blankets entangling my body like a man struggling to escape a straight-jacket. The black cat didn't care. It stubbornly sat there, motionless on my chest, gazing at me as if it was in a cat trance, unaffected by the annoying ring tone. It's perfect natural balance rendered it impervious to my movement.

"You're not the boss of me." I yelled at the annoying mouser.

It ignored my defiance.

Did it want to kill me and eat me? Did it have some other nefarious plot in the works? I don't even like cats. Cats are known to lie and are notoriously evil. Why was it here? Are cats aliens? I read that somewhere.

My mind, gradually shifting now from drunken dozing to a more vigilant mode, sent me an emergency message.

Coffee... must have coffee... otherwise certain death is imminent...

I tried to remember if I purchased more coffee at the store last trip.

A cough and wheeze interrupted my thoughts... mornings are so confusing.

I ignored the incoming phone call. Sitting up in bed, I carefully guided the obnoxious cat off my chest. No sense in getting clawed to death... slow and careful is the name of the game with a dangerous animal. "Nice kitty... please move or I will shoot you."

Stupid cat. It's not even mine. I think it knows the

gun is out of reach. Is it smirking? Can a cat smirk? Why don't they respect personal space?

It was time to dispense some cat discipline. I gave it my old police-trainer face and growled at it. "Cat, you don't live here. What are you doing here? You should go home."

By the time I finally worked up the nerve to challenge its trespassing and invasion of personal space, the black cat turned away and flopped down at the foot of the bed, falling immediately asleep on its back with all four paws in the air. I don't think it heard me... or did it? I don't think it cared either way. Why did it wake me up if it didn't want anything? Cats are officially not my favorite animal.

I found some clean enough old sweatpants on the back of a chair, tugged them on, and staggered into the kitchen to make a pot of the Black Death. My expensive drip coffee maker with the swanky integrated bean grinder was broken... It quit working about eight months ago. Perhaps enough time has passed to make it officially broken forever. But it cost a lot of money, so I'd leave it sit there a few more months before I would toss it in the dumpster out back. Luckily, my old drip coffee-maker still worked. There was some ground coffee stashed in the cupboard from last Christmas, so I engineered a filter out of a cocktail napkin I pilfered from the corner bar a while back and dumped some in it. Next some water... then hit the red button and soon, coffee... delicious coffee. Life-sustaining coffee.

I went to the bathroom to take care of business while the pot percolated or whatever coffee pots do. I think it is percolate.

By the time I came out of the head, my coffee-like substance was ready. The cat was now making some cat noises while circling the front of the fridge. I blasted it with another half-hearted scolding while I poured myself a cup.

"What do you want? You don't live here. You should go home."

No response.

Meowing continues.

"I shouldn't feed you. You aren't my cat. I don't have any cats. All those cats that I don't have include you."

Continued meowing ensued.

I found a little airliner-size bottle of Baileys behind the brick of cheese and a mooshed up stick of butter on the refrigerator door, so I poured milk-like liqueur in a bowl and tossed in a chip of butter in a bowl. Well, it wasn't exactly a bowl. It was a red plastic cup I shortened to cat-size with some scissors. I don't have a bowl.

The cat hunkered over its gourmet cat breakfast, greedily lapping up Baileys, its back arched like it was defending a kill... at least it wasn't meowing now, so that's nice.

I poured some more Joe in my 'Old Salt 'coffee cup and initiated a search for my smart phone. If I recall, it was ringing earlier in the vicinity of the bedroom. After checking the two or three places I normally leave it after an evening of debauchery, I found the phone stuffed in the pocket of last night's pants, which were wadded up in a pile of other clothes in the corner. I think I might have undressed angry, or maybe drunk… or maybe drunk and angry.

Don't worry. It's fine. I'm a professional… uh, this is something I'm trained to handle.

Blinking my bloodshot peepers, I stared into the phone screen long enough for it to finally come into focus. A missed a call from an unknown number and… oh crap… my asshole cousin, Johnny Deddario, an ex-cop turned professional goon, known on the street as Johnny Dedd left a voice mail.

I made the executive decision to ignore the call. He was family, but he was also bad news. We used to be members of the same police department, but Johnny was fired from the force for murdering an unarmed child molester. He did a stretch in prison for it, too. Then I think he became a bagman for hoods, collecting bills and enforcing the terms of violated loan agreements with extreme violence. He always seems to have plenty of money, so I guess he's doing okay.

Nothing good ever comes from dealing with Johnny, except perhaps that time a few months ago when he blew away the hitman who was about to whack me in Chinatown. But he also once had a relationship with my ex-girlfriend, which pisses me off. But it was before she was my girlfriend, so I can't be too angry. He was about the only family I had left, so I don't hate him, but I don't seek opportunities to interact with him. He's violent and dangerous, perhaps a psychopath. I'm peaceful and safe, totally not a psychopath. We have nothing in common.

Speaking of violent and dangerous, I needed to get to the office early this morning to meet with Mister Stump, my finance manager, business associate, and life coach. Mister Stump was a hood, a bagman for organized crime elements, although mostly retired. He's good with numbers, smart with money, and generous with advice that often sounds suspiciously like criticism. He's also extremely violent. But we share an office and he seldom hurts me unless he feels like it. We had a nice little score on a recent gig, so our business and personal relationship had been pretty positive lately.

I got cleaned up, put on a nice black suit and clasped my Rolex Submariner 5512 to my wrist. It was vintage but still had good lume. I dropped my black Sinatra classic dress hat on my head. I had to admit, I looked sharp.

"Cat, do I look sharp, or what? I asked.

The cat ignored me. It was stretched out on my coffee table. The stupid trespasser wasn't moving. Was it dead?

"Cat... hey!"

Nobody wants a dead cat on his coffee table. I

scratched its ear to confirm it was deceased. It returned the gesture with one slight and casual tail wag with a whisker twitch on the side. I guess it wasn't dead.

"You're in charge until I get back, asshole."

The cat sat up and licked its butt. In cat language, that is the equivalent of a salute to a superior officer and an acknowledgement of a direct order. Full disclosure, I don't speak cat language.

The weather report said damp and chilly, so I grabbed my Burberry trench coat from of the closet on the way out.

I locked up my apartment and hopped into the Mustang. The cat could find its own way out.

It was time for Joe Tucker to go to work.

Who is Joe Tucker, you ask? That's me...

I'm Joe Tucker, ex-hero cop, critically injured in the line of duty, currently operating as a licensed private investigator in the State of California. Within my Stefano Ricci crocodile wallet, I have a private nose ticket and a license to pack a roscoe. I consider myself an emerging entrepreneur in the business world. I enjoy reading business and investment news, although my only investments to date have been my Rolex Submariner and cat food. I dress well from my post-police days as a high-end department store detective where I had a generous employee discount... I like to look good and I appreciate nice things. Do I have a penchant for luxury items that I cannot really afford? Yes, guilty as charged. But I don't have a cat. The black fur-devil on my coffee table is my neighbor's cat. It is not a luxury item.

Tucker Investigations Agency, LLC—Downtown Los Angeles

I parked in the basement garage and took the lucky pre-world-war-two elevator to my floor. I scooted through the narrow little hall that led to the office door of Tucker Investigations LLC.

I listened for a minute, I always do, to try to identify if any trouble was waiting for me inside.

Nothing.

I slowly opened the door a crack and was welcomed to a whiff of Gentilli Deli burps and cigar smoke. My life coach and financial advisor was in.

I found Mister Stump in his designated spot on the couch, looking like three-hundred-pounds of lumpy white gravy over a big biscuit in a pale green polyester suit, white socks, and mailman shoes. He sported a pork-pie hat that was screwed on his head like he was born wearing it.

"Good morning," I said as I stepped through the door and made my way past his bulk to my desk.

He was busy scribbling in a little notebook with the stub of a number two pencil. He looked up long enough to flip me off with a fat middle finger. I noticed his knuckles were bruised. He also had a nice manicure, which seemed incongruent with his early 1970s style of dress. But Mister Stump is a series of contradictions wrapped in a skin bag of ugly. I said nothing. Still the skinned up knuckles were odd. He usually uses the brass knuckles in his pants pockets if he needs to help someone recall an overdue bill.

I'm a medically retired police detective, so I notice the little things. It's called being a trained observer.

"How did you bruise your knuckles, Mister Stump? Did you have to punch some poor gambler over a delinquent twenty-dollar debt?"

He didn't look up. "No… it was an accident," he grumbled as he continued with his writing and doing his best to ignore me.

"No kidding?" That was a legitimate surprise. I can't envision Mister Stump having accidents. He causes accidents… usually on purpose. Some medical researchers suggest he might be the number one cause of broken legs in the metro-Los Angeles area.

"Yeah, I was slamming some guy's head in a car door and got my hand caught in the way. It's sad really. Did you know that if you are a private contractor, you can't file an industrial injury claim?"

"Yeah, that *is* sad." Agreeing with Mister Stump is always a good idea.

My phone rang again. I pulled it out of my pocket to see who it was this time… and it was my cousin again.

"Aw shit."

My meager obscenity caught the attention of Mister Stump.

"What are you aw shitting about?" he grunted, again without looking up.

"It's my cousin."

That news caught his attention. "Johnny Dedd? He's good people. I like him," Stump commented in his bullfrog voice.

I called him out on this obvious blasphemy. "Bullshit, Stump... you hate everybody. You're just saying that to piss me off."

"So?"

I wasn't sure what to say to that. I went with the truth. "It worked... I'm pissed off."

"Good... but I *do* like that guy," Stump grumbled, as he returned to his calculations, or whatever the hell he was doing. Maybe he was writing a list of the people who needed broken legs today.

Against my better judgment, I took the phone call.

"Tucker Investigations. Joe Tucker speaking," I said in my professional voice, casually looking at my watch as I spoke, to reflect my total lack of interest in Johnny Dedd, the womanizing lech. Even though he couldn't see my act of disinterest, he had to sense it.

My cousin Johnny is a vain Italian womanizer. He can't get over how handsome he thinks he is... even with the bent beak he picked up recently. But women inevitably like me better once they get to know me. I'm better looking than he is and I don't have a prison sentence on my resume. Also, I'm charming. Why girls slobber over him like fleas on a stray dog is beyond me... if fleas slobber. I don't know that they do. They might. Fleas just are tiny flies, right? I don't know if flies slobber either. Let's just say women go crazy over him for no reason and it sort of pisses me off.

"Joe, it's Cousin Johnny."

Nothing good ever comes from a discussion with Johnny. Did I mention he used to date my girl? I mean, my ex-girl... Asshole.

"I can't talk now, Johnny... I have a very important client in the office," I lied.

Stump uttered an extended version of the word 'bullshit' from across the room, loud enough to be picked up over the phone. Stump is a dick. I'm not sure that Johnny heard him rat me out or even cared if he *did* hear it. Johnny is one of those guys who go through life with little introspection, no shame, and zero regrets. I've never understood how you can live in LA and not be at least a little neurotic. Guys like Johnny and Stump manage it, though.

Dedd pressed with an unusual urgency in his tone, like a cop calling 'shots fired 'over a radio. "Joe, shut the fuck up and listen. It's Joan Vance. She got shot earlier this morning. I'm coming in hot from Calabasas. Get curbside in five and I'll pick you up on the way to the hospital."

"Fuck."

I never got over Joan, even though I seldom think about her or talk about her... much. Last time I saw her was at her place of employment. She frisked me, slapped me, kissed me, and then threw me out of the Beverly Hills Police Department like I was some random skid-row bum, even though I was legitimately investigating the murder of rich kid from Florida.

I believe she still has feelings for me. I mean, she didn't kill me on sight. That's how I can tell that all her old romantic feelings are still alive.

I snapped back to the present.

"Is she alive?"

"As far as I know."

I'm heading downstairs now," I growled into the phone, then disconnected. I was numb. *Joan was shot? How? Why?*

Shocking news never seems real. It seems like something you are hearing about that happened to someone you never heard of, someone in a far away land you will probably never visit. I keep saying 'never' as I try to process it. I guess the word 'never' explains it best as in 'I never thought this would happen.'

Stump gave me a 'whiskey tango foxtrot' look.

I gave the news to him down and dirty. "Joan Vance got shot. Johnny is picking me up on the way to the hospital."

"Dead?"

"Still alive."

He didn't hesitate. "I'm going with you."

Stump followed me out as I locked the deadbolt on the rickety wood and glass office door. We made our way to the street hustling down the stairs as fast as his bad knees and my damaged lungs would carry us. The creaking steps were faster than waiting for the ancient pre-World War Two elevator to arrive and take us down the three floors to the street.

I give Stump credit, if there is action, the ancient mobster blob wants to be there, and I find comfort in having the sadistic brute on my side when the shit hits the fan. Besides, he always seemed to like Joan, but probably because she dumped me.

In just shy of three minutes, a hulking black 1970 Cadillac DeVille Convertible came screaming around the corner with its top down, coming to a skidding stop at the curb in front of our building. The big boat's paint glistened with the thin coating of moisture lingering in the air, the ghostly yellow glow caused more from street lights than sunlight in the eternal darkness that is L.A. right now. I wasn't surprised he had the top down, in spite of the biting chill in the air. Johnny rarely puts the top up on his baby unless he's parking it on the street and out of his immediate sight for more than three minutes. Smart people, car people, street people, hoods, and cops don't molest Johnny Dedd's car because they like living. But LA has an abundance of stupid people. So he takes appropriate security precautions to avoid having to kill those assholes later should they screw up and touch his precious automobile.

Stump smiled, "Nice wheels." He turned and

addressed me, "You don't see Johnny Dedd driving a piece of shit little car. Dedd appreciates the big classics made for real men. He has some class." Then the big moose gingerly hopped over the side and plopped into the back seat like a teenager.

How does he do that? He's like a hundred years old or something... plus obese and ugly.

I ignored his cheap shot about my car, which I prefer to Johnny's old gas guzzling beast, and slid into the front passenger seat. My decade old Mustang convertible was just as cool, in my opinion.

I felt the four-barrel carburetor kick in as Johnny stomped on the accelerator. In an instant, we were flying towards the hospital like a big 747 blasting down a runway, taking off or landing, your choice. My eyes were closed. Johnny is a highly-trained pursuit operations driver but unfortunately, he drives like a highly-trained pursuit operations driver.

Stump complimented Johnny on his car again. "Beautiful ride, Johnny. You can't go wrong with a..."

We were here for Joan, not a car club cruise-in. I cut him off. "How is she? What happened?"

Johnny talked and drove, his face as grim and taut as a constipated winner of a hot dog eating contest. "Not good. They took her to the Harbor-UCLA Medical Center. All I know is that she was assigned to the LA County organized crime task force surveillance."

"The one LAPD and the Bureau runs?" Stump

asked.

"Yeah, she's been there a while," Johnny answered. "They were tailing some Yakuza gangster into the commercial docks at the harbor, but it was an ambush. Her partner is dead. She was hit a few times. That's all I know."

"How did you hear about it?"

"Her mom called me," he explained.

"Her mom? Called you?" I asked... this was a startling development.

"We used to date," he said as dispassionately as a normal person mentioning they once saw a tree.

Did I just hear that? Are those words supposed to go together to make a sentence that a human being would say?

I shook off the worst of my shock. "What the hell? You dated her mom too?"

That is just a whole new level of disgusting.

"Just for a while," he continued as nonchalantly as if he was providing a weather report. "When Joan dumped me for messing around with another woman for the third time, her mom demanded to pick up the slack. You know how that always happens when you date a woman. You usually end up dating her mother too at some point."

"What the hell?"

My brain went on overload. *Why didn't Joan's mom ever call me? Did she remember me? Joan and I were almost engaged. I'm not sure I ever mentioned that to her. Even so, she had to know. Joan must talk about me all the time... right?*

"What the hell?" I said again, answering my own obsessive thoughts aloud.

Johnny's answer snapped me out of my reverie. "You already said that once. What's your point?"

I tried to elucidate, even though I knew explaining anything to Johnny about normal human interaction was pointless. "Nobody ever dates somebody's mom when they break up, Johnny... it's not a thing that happens. In fact, it's obscene."

The point went through one of his ears and out the other without ever making contact with a brain cell.

"Oh, it got kind of obscene all right. Very obscene." He added wistfully with a cruel yet charming smile. Then he turned to me with his oddly serious rationalization. "But I'm not a kiss and tell, Joe. Besides, I have to spread this Italian charm around. It's like a responsibility."

Johnny has zero comprehension of what Joan and I had together before I messed it up. He isn't being a dick. My cousin spent his whole life as a guy with hordes of women throwing themselves at him, and for him that is simply his normal world. Still, it pissed me off. I'm just as handsome and I don't dress in a lot of black leather shit like some B-Movie super-villain. Unlike Johnny, I dress for success... I used to work loss-prevention at the most elite department store in Los Angeles. I had the employee discount. I pride myself on my clothes and appearance. Plus, that nose of his looks like he tried to catch a concrete block with his face.

It was time to clear the air. "You *know* we were engaged…" I said with more disgust in my voice than intended. Well, to be candid, maybe I intended more disgust.

Johnny was nonplused by my emotional heartfelt revelation. "Not when I dated her, cousin. What can I say? How can that be my fault? Besides, you were never legally engaged. You just told people you were engaged. In fact, you told everyone but her, dumbass."

Stump intervened, using his gift of diplomacy and a 1911 Colt he pulled from a belt holster. He swung the big automatic over the seat, suggestively waving it back and forth between us, while posing a stern warning. "Shut up, you assholes."

I don't think Stump is comfortable with family bickering or any musings about romance and broken hearts. He's happier not talking at all. He enjoys breaking legs and bookkeeping. I don't think he has a lot of friends.

The passenger compartment remained quiet for the rest of the trip.

Stump seemed happy.

Harbor-UCLA Medical Center

As we pulled into the parking lot, I felt my anxiety levels raging in an upward spiral. But not about Joan or the wild high-speed ride through LA with crazy Johnny at the wheel. It was all about our destination coming into full view. I was on the verge of a full-blown panic attack. I had too much hospital time in my history.

Seeing the cold stone building and hearing an ambulance siren whining down the road, I flashed back to my career-ending injuries and subsequent year-long recovery in a hospital just like this one.

It happened back when I was still a cop working patrol division. I went off duty around two in the morning. On my way home, I made a life-changing decision.

I decided to make a stop on the way home.

I wheeled into a twenty-four-hour convenience market to grab some beer and a bag of potato chips. I missed my lunch break during shift and didn't feel like preparing a meal, not that I'm much of a cook anyway. Chips and beer would get me by.

My head was totally up my ass. Some call it fat, dumb, and happy. Cops call it condition white.

I wore my policeman's tuxedo that night; the 'after-shift 'dark blue uniform pants and white t-shirt with a Velcro belt and black SWAT style boots. My uniform shirt was locked away securely in the trunk with my war-bag and rifle. I'll freely admit that I don't know whom my outfit was supposed to fool. It should be obvious to anyone that I was a cop. In retrospect, I should have pulled on the Hawaiian shirt I kept in the backseat, but I was too lazy. Doing so might have bought me a few seconds of reaction time I would soon desperately need. My poor judgment and lack of situational awareness would cost me a lung.

My duty weapon, an old-school four-inch barreled Model 13 Smith, was stuffed in my belt, obviously imprinted under my t-shirt.

The clerk was a Sikh guy. He was visibly agitated. That was a sign. Sikhs don't get agitated. They are warriors by nature. His subtle distress was an obvious sign. I should have picked up on it. I'm a professional. We are supposed to notice these things and make reasonable conclusions. I did neither.

At the time, I was probably in the best physical condition of my life. I was a SWAT team member, a defensive tactics instructor, and I worked out and ran every day. That disciplined regimen might have been what kept me alive for the next five minutes.

But I had my head up my ass.

I didn't pay attention to the car backed into the parking space in front of the doors with some salty-looking nimrod behind the wheel, just like I didn't pick up on the clerk's anxiety. I was grooving on the smell of those rotating hot dogs and the toxic chemicals they use to clean the floor. I don't know why I love the smell of a convenience store.

I believe I previously mentioned my head was up my ass. It bears repeating.

Anyone with professional experience will recognize the series of fuck-ups I've just delineated. Yet, from time to time, all of us still do stupid shit like this. Condition white. Clueless. Rectal-cranial inversion. Call it what you will, you already know what I did wrong. If you never came off a long shift, tired and hungry, and walked into a familiar convenience store with your head up your ass, then you are a liar. I don't want to hear the lectures. I know I screwed up.

I walked in and did the condition white stare, my head wobbling around on my neck like a tourist from Booger County Mississippi laying eyes on the Empire State Building for the first time. I knew where everything in that store was shelved. I'd been in there a million times. But I still had to stop and look around in my confused and shift-fatigued foggy state.

Asshole number one stepped from behind a rack of sunglasses. He was wearing a red bandana over his face and had a shotgun in his hands at the low ready. For an asshole, he had good body mechanics. He shuffle-stepped, shifted, and butt-stroked me in the face, knocking out a bunch of my teeth and knocking me flat on my ass.

That sensation haunts me to this day, in a relentlessly cruel way. Even now, every time I walk into a store, I feel it. I briefly obsess about that time I got clocked with the gun butt and how it felt swallowing my own teeth. The coppery taste of warm blood overflowed in my mouth and I almost choked on it. I remember the viscous red fluid running down the front of my white t-shirt. I remember rolling off my back, instinctively laboring to get to all fours, and trying to remember where in the hell I was and what just happened to me.

But my training kicked in. As the bad guy

racked the shotgun to finish me, I intuitively pulled my revolver.

My draw was blindingly fast. I had rehearsed grasping my weapon and firing thousands of times at the police range. I had even practiced a draw and dry-fire at home at least a few times a week. I snaked the gun out and put the front sight on him faster than the human brain could process. Instinctual movement, muscle memory, sight picture… I remember the robber's facial expression as he realized what was happening. His countenance transfigured from a bloodthirsty murderer to a fresh kid witnessing a magic trick and not believing his eyes. I pumped three screaming hot thirty-eight caliber +P rounds into his center of mass. My senses were on fire. I could almost see the hollow points expand as they ripped holes in his chest. I watched his ten ring turn bright red.

He felt it.

Only seconds prior, I thought I was a dead man. Now, I knew I had a chance to survive the incident, that's what I call it now, the incident. My training carried me through and kept me alive.

It was then that shotgun boy's buddy, who had been standing down an aisle to my left between the cereal and motor oil, shot me. He was the asshole I hadn't seen yet. It's always the 'asshole you don't see yet' who gets you. He got me. The tweaked-out bastard dumped three rounds into my chest.

At that moment, I learned what a collapsed

lung felt like. I couldn't breathe. I thought I might be dead. But I kept going.

Our range master at the police department, Scott, was a tough old bastard, a former-Marine. I don't believe he had a first name. He was born without a neck or wrists, just a burly torso with a big block head screwed on it. He didn't have normal arms. Scott had big meaty jackhammers with hams for fists at the end of the beefy, thick appendages. His legs were like old growth forest timber. His feet measured in at 11.5 triple wide. His big ass was as broad as a dump truck. Scott was a man. Perhaps prehistoric, but still a man's man.

He drilled us constantly on fighting our way through fear and never quitting. A lot of people in the upper levels of the police department didn't like it. A few rank-climbing officers who's idea of police work was attending the Mayor's community breakfast sessions to bitch about real cops, didn't like it either. They all believed Scott's way was overkill which would lead to excessive force complaints. On the street, an excessive force complaint is what pussies make when they lose a fight. These so-called leaders and wanna-be leaders undermined Scott's lessons at every opportunity. I wasn't one of those people. I absorbed his drills like a sponge.

And now those lessons would be put to the ultimate test.

A lot of officers often find themselves outnumbered and out-gunned in their careers. Whether they live or die depends on guys like our range master. His way wasn't pretty. In fact, it was butt ugly, but it saved the lives of many officers. I remembered the other guys who claimed his lessons saved their lives. That helped to me carry on while I was facing imminent death. I was just as good a cop as those others and I didn't have to die at the hands of assholes today. And even if I *did* lose, the assholes would know they'd been in a fight.

Now it was my turn to hold fast for the thin blue line.

I was groggy but still functioning. Unable to form a sight-picture, I point-fired my remaining three rounds in the cylinder at him. One caught him in the knee. Another in the throat. I don't know where the other round went.

He fell.

The Sikh clerk leaped across the counter and started stomping on him like he was putting out a fire. He went berserk on that piece of shit. It made me glad we were on the same team.

Things were looking up. Then they weren't.

I had a second to wonder if the clerk remembered to hit the alarm before he hopped over the counter and joined the fray. Some back-up for the good guys would be nice right now. I didn't want to die bleeding out on the floor of a convenience store.

About that time, the asshole from the backed-in car came in looking for his pals.

I forgot about him.

I was out of ammo. I had no more rounds. The spares were in my duty belt in the trunk. I never thought I'd need more than six... or ten... or thirty rounds... nobody thinks they will need more rounds until they need more rounds.

Car guy ran inside and drop kicked me hard in the side. It hurt. In case you don't know, getting kicked in the side after you had the living shit shot out of you really hurts. It's quite demoralizing. But I wasn't ready to quit. I wanted to live. More importantly, I wanted to kill every one of these rat bastards, even if it was my last act on this planet.

In combat, fighting spirit, rage, and hatred will keep you alive longer than prayer and reflection. Prayer and reflection are for the survivors or the dying. Not bashing the value of my religious upbringing, but when shit is on the line, rowing away from the rocks will keep you alive longer than praying that the boat doesn't sink.

Full disclosure, I might have prayed a little while I was sucking air down my blood-filled throat.

I rolled with his kick and continued rolling over to a beer display, trying to create some reactive space to stage a defense.

He charged at me like a madman, taking a skip-hop and lifting his foot to deliver a fatal stomp on my throat. I don't know if he had a firearm, but he was about to murder me, so I didn't care.

I might not be a highly educated man, but there was a singular fact of which I was certain.

One of us would die in that store within the next thirty seconds.

I spun clockwise on my hip, knocking his back foot out from under him with a sweeping kick from the ground, just as his heavy-heeled Doc Martin style boot came down on its way to murder me. With one of his feet off the floor, my kick to his supporting ankle made him tumble, spin, and fall on his back, landing on the floor beside me.

I don't know if I delivered a good kick or if he was just higher than a kite and extremely clumsy. The results were the same, and I saw my chance to live. I spit what felt like a gallon of foamy blood out of my mouth and went on offense.

Grabbing a twelve-pack of Natty Light from the display to my right, I got to my knees and beat him to death with it.

I swung down hard.

On the third hit, the twelve-pack came apart. A dozen beers flew across the store, exploding and spraying foam, sacrificing their lives in the furtherance of justice.

I grabbed another twelve pack. This one held together better. I got at least twenty hits in with it, holding on to the twelve-pack's cardboard handle like a war-hammer.

I repeatedly smashed his head with that one until the counterman finally pulled me off.

He told me in heavily accented English that the guy he had been pounding into the linoleum floor had finally succumbed to my earlier gunfire, and it was all over.

I heard the back-ups rolling hot in response to the silent alarm.

He *did* remember to hit the alarm.

"You will be okay, officer. They are coming," he tried to reassure me. He put a nasty counter rag over the worst of my wounds. Not only did this patriot save my life, but now I'll probably be immune to all germs. Once you mix your blood with a convenience store counter rag, that immunity lasts forever.

I heard his words and felt reassured. I felt like I was going to make it. I experienced that sensation you get when you think you are going to die, but you don't. I was giddy... everything was funny. That survival high left me tripping like a happy drunk.

"Thanks dude... I owe you man... You fight good."

"I'm an American. It was my job," he replied proudly. He popped open a bloody beer can from the twelve-pack and handed it to me, then grabbed on for himself. I'm not sure if that violated their religious code, but I'm pretty sure their version of the pope, whoever he or she might be, would give him a pass on it.

Sikhs rock.

I took the beer and smiled at him with no teeth. Then I started to pass out in a growing pool of my own frothy blood. I never got to enjoy my free beer.

He appeared confused.

I'm not sure he knew I smiled. He might have thought I just died. I don't think I looked like a picture of good health.

The world did a fade to black.

Later they told me I croaked in the meat wagon and the medics brought me back. I don't recall seeing a white light, and if I did, I was in no condition to walk towards it.

Then there was a year in the hospital... a year of probes, pricks, and the removal of most of a severely damaged lung. Then the department medically retired me with a nice pension, a payout for workers compensation, and a friendly handshake as they saw me to the door.

"Where the hell did you go?" Stump asked as he shook my shoulder. "You zoned completely out."

Shit, it was happening again, the old PTSD... Picturing Terrible Shit Daily or whatever it stands for... The lost time, intensely bright colored recollection, completely phased out of the present... dammit.

I provided a feeble explanation. "Sorry, not a fan of hospitals. Let's go."

"Puss," he muttered.

We made our way through security and found an ER nurses' station. In retrospect, I guess we were a shifty-looking crew, a retired hero-cop, a convict ex-cop, and an aging hood.

I caught the attention of a middle-aged nurse who appeared to have seen too much in her medical career and probably went around the bend mentally at some point. She was now relegated to reception where she could do no more damage. She was a dinosaur who probably was quite comfortable amputating body parts all day or smothering people who annoyed her with pillows. I've seen combat veterans with that stare in their eyes. She was a stocky woman but appeared to have once been quite attractive at the beginning of her medical profession sojourn. Her nameplate said Nurse Slaughter, which was an unfortunate surname for a medical professional.

"We're looking for Joan Vance," I announced professionally, with a hint of authority. All cops have a hint of authority in their voice, even when they aren't cops anymore.

"Family only." She grunted as she turned her attention back to paperwork and placed us on ignore.

I noticed the Operation Desert Storm tattoo on her inner forearm. She noticed that I noticed. I started to say something about veterans but she gave me that look that says, don't even think about going there.

Johnny gave me a nudge and moved into the pole position.

"Nurse. We *are* family... well, almost family... by the way, do *you* have family? Like a husband? I'm single... I love nurses. Scrubs are a total turn on... Did you know that? They really are. That dark blue color you have is particularly attractive."

He released a registered Johnny Dedd charm smile on the poor woman. It was the smile that never fails, the smile that allows him to get away with almost anything. No woman has resistance to that smile, no matter how crude or obnoxious he might be, nor how lame his pickup lines sound... except maybe this time.

The nurse delivered a merciless glare so cold and heartless that it could knock a cockroach off a shit house after discount night at the Golden Corral. "Forget it Romeo. You need to step back or I'm calling security."

She reached for an unknown object in the purse beside her chair... probably a chain saw.

Our reception nurse was immune to Johnny's charm. I thought from the look on his face he might cry. He was in shock. His eyes watered a little but didn't form a tear. I felt bad for him. His ego is quite frail in these matters.

Stump elbowed his way between us, bulling through like a hog that just spotted a watermelon rind.

He subtly softened his usually gruff voice, sounding less like his normal grinding gear in an off-balance concrete mixer and more like a well-tuned diesel engine on a tug boat. "Lady, we *are* her family. We're going in. Anybody tries to stop us; I'll personally beat their sorry asses senseless... then you *will* have a busy night at your little hospital. Got it, lady?"

I'm pretty sure he added an eyebrow wiggle,

softening his threat... or maybe some of his forehead skin came loose from his skull. That is a thing that sometimes happens to old people I hear. Well, I haven't actually heard it. I just made that up. But it makes sense.

Nurse Slaughter got the message... Her glare softened ever so slightly and she waved us through without another word.

Stump grabbed Johnny and me by the arms and marched us towards the ICU like a junior-high principal marching a couple of wise-ass eighth-graders to the principal's office.

I swear I heard the Nurse Slaughter stage whisper with a hint of poorly concealed admiration, "Finally, a real man," as we made our way to the ICU.

Joan's mom, sitting in a tasteless snot green armless plastic chair that seemed to be designed for discomfort and ugliness, was the only person in the cold featureless hallway outside Joan's hospital room. That seemed strange. Officers are supposed to be assigned to security when a cop gets shot. There should be a uniformed officer at the door and an officer at the entrance to the ward. I could see Joan inside the glass box of an ICU room, wrapped up in bandages, slings, and partially concealed among various pieces of medical technology.

The lights, machines, and noises made me feel like I might pass out. I could smell the disgusting antiseptic odor permeating through my nostrils, that unmistakeable hospital smell became over-whelming. My breathing was shallow and acceler-ated. I felt myself getting lightheaded again. I hate hospitals.

Unwelcome anxiety had its big hairy paws around my throat and was choking me out.

I started consciously trying to control each breath, slowing down my heartbeat and lowering my blood pressure. This place was rubbing fear and dread into every pore of my body like a Texan smearing seasoning on a brisket, but I fought off the panic. I only have about fifty percent breathing capacity since I got shot, so I am at risk of passing out under stress most of the time even in the best conditions. My doctors require me to remain calm, at least as calm as possible given my job. I have a low-key personality, unlike my cousin, which helps.

Joan's mother smiled at the sight of us, rose from her seat, and gave Johnny Dedd a sloppy kiss on the lips that lasted a little longer than appropri-ate, considering he used to date her daughter. Now I admit, her mom is hot for her age, no denying it. She is a total cougar. But she is also like twenty-five years older than us. But she was hot, so...

After they ended the creepy lip lock, she shook my hand with all the affection of a banker who just unilaterally closed your overdrawn account. The lack of warmth was annoying and hurtful. But she never really liked me that much anyway, as far as I know. Still, this was about Joan, not me. Joan was her daughter and even if you are a shitty parent who kisses Johnny Dedd, that still means something in times of crisis. She was polite to me, but unnecessarily chilly considering how close I came to being her son-in-law... if I had ever told Joan we were engaged... and if she had accepted... and if everything had worked out according to my unrealistic fantasies.

Her mom went directly to the point, speaking to my cousin first. "Thanks for coming, Johnny." She turned her attention to me, "Joan asked for you. I'm not sure why. She just said, find Joe."

"Really?"

I didn't see that coming. For a moment, I felt a burst of excitement at the possibility of Joan wanting me beside her in a time of dire need. But as much as I wanted to explore that phenomenon, I had higher tier security concerns on my mind. As lovesick as I am over her, her safety trumps everything else. I may be a dumbass, but I always get the job done, and the job was protecting Joan.

I refocused and asked Joan's mom a question. "Where are the cops? Why aren't they guarding her?"

She looked at me a bit softer, like I wasn't a disgusting parasite. "There were two here, but twenty minutes ago they were pulled off to help guard the suspects. Two of the guys they caught were shot up pretty bad and are downstairs getting treated. Joan's boss felt the highest potential threat was if a group of the suspects 'allies, whoever that is, showed up here at the hospital to extract them. Or worse, I suppose. He told me that was the best way to protect her. Then he left and never came back. I don't like him much... I can tell you that!"

Stump grunted, "That's bullshit. If it was one of ours, there would be three heavily armed goombahs at each end of the hall and a torpedo in the room with her to keep the doctors in line."

She seemed confused, yet titillated. "Us? Goombahs?"

I don't think Joan's mom speaks 'mob' but she obviously liked the sound of it.

My colleague introduced himself. "The name is Stump, madam. We are here to help you and your daughter. My services are at your disposal."

She shook his hand, hanging on to his big greasy gorilla paw for a period of time I once again felt was longer than appropriate. She introduced herself to Stump. "I'm Deb Deluca... married name, of course. I *am* divorced."

She did the *'I'm divorced'* shrug and smile combo, which is an intimate non-verbal version of *'welcome aboard.* 'She left off her full 'name-resume' which was more like Deb Ford-Chevy-Buick-Dodge-Deluca... if memory serves, which it doesn't. I think she has been married five or six times. Not judging... She certainly had a lot to offer a man and she found men to be interchangeable collector's items. She could get away with it, because she was hot. Not to me of course, but to older men and perverts like Johnny Dedd.

Stump responded by taking her tiny manicured diamond and gold jewelry littered hand, lifted it to his gorilla-like face, and kissed it.

I almost puked. I've never seen him act that way before. Of course, I seldom see him other than when he is on the office couch being pissed off or when we are out on a case and he is beating people senseless while being pissed off. The common denominator in all of his behavior is 'pissed off.' It's difficult for me to picture him as a real person interacting with other real people and not being pissed off.

Stump spoke to her using actual words instead of his usual 'old gangster 'jargon. "As I said before, Deb, May I call you Deb?"

She assumed that provocative stance women take when they insinuate you should check out the goods. I felt like puking again, but didn't... yet.

"Why certainly, Mister Stump. I would like that very much," she cooed.

He continued his lame bullshit. "As I said before, I am at your service, Miss Deluca. My staff and I will help on this case in anyway we can."

When did he learn to be civilized? Is he evolving into something else? Is he learning our human ways and customs in order to conquer us? And what is this 'my staff 'bullshit? If anyone is in charge here, it's me.

Deb's body language continued to demonstrate a deep appreciation of Stump's approach. She orbited a little closer to his gravitational pull. "Thank you so much, Mister Stump. You have *no* idea how comforting it is to have such an obviously competent man like you offer his assistance." She ran her hand up and down the back of his arm as she spoke.

My mind was still spinning at his last line of bullshit. Staff? What the hell? We're not his staff. Did he mean us? Or did he mean the mob? This isn't good. And why did she call him competent? I am competent too... after all, I was almost her son-in-law... well, not almost, but it was possible. Where do they get off with this crap? What does Stump think he's trying to pull?

I cleared my throat and interjected myself back into the conversation. I'm the only legally certified 'hero' here. It was time to assert my rightful place as leader of this team. "Uh, we're *all* here to help, Miss Deluca. What happened? Can you tell us more?"

She kept making eyes at Stump as she spoke to me. "The police won't share much with me, but I think this is bigger than it appears." Her face hardened with her voice as she now turned her full attention to me. "Call me paranoid, Tucker, but I think her team was set up... probably by someone in the police department or city hall... or higher."

I frowned. I saw a frown appear on Johnny's face too. He might have been sent to prison for the sins he committed as a cop, like murder for example, but he wasn't crooked. He is just an extremely violent but likable psychopath. He despised police corruption as much as I did. With the exception of his proclivity for murdering perverts, he had been a great cop.

Stump asked her, "What makes you say that?" The old mobster's interest seemed piqued at the possibility of corrupt cops turning on their own.

Joan's mom continued, "I overheard one of them tell their boss that 'it happened again...' whatever that means... and every blue suit and trench coat in the joint has been in the silent cold-shoulder mode around us. Usually when a cop gets hurt in the line of duty, they have public relations guys and assistant police chiefs out there soaking up as much pity as possible from the public. You've seen it on TV before too, I'm sure... but this? This response is like a secret CIA operation gone bad... we aren't getting any help or information from the department... and..." her voice cracked, "That's my little girl in there."

I saw the tell-tale chin tremble. I knew the faucets were about to be turned on.

Deb began sobbing, the hard veneer of the tough sexy divorcee' washed away by a mother's tears. Stump gently put his arm around her shoulders and walked Deb over to a broken down old black leather couch further down the white florescent hall. They sat down together as she continued crying uncontrollably, burying her head into his meaty shoulder. It was weird seeing that big mug comforting another human being. To him, comforting someone usually means putting them out of their misery. I haven't seen this side of Mister

Stump before.

We ended up killing most of the day, waiting for something to happen. Before we knew it the sun was going down again.

Johnny and I huddled up outside the door of Joan's room. We were out of earshot from Deb and Stump, who were seated near the exit.

"What do you think?" I asked, really wanting to know what my cousin made of what Deb had told us. His street senses were attuned to a level that was almost superhuman. For a dumbass murdering psycho, he was clever and intuitive. Johnny Dedd doesn't survive you, he makes you survive him.

I didn't feel any competition between Johnny and I over Joan would be a factor in working on this together. He was over Joan in a romantic sense, but once you are a friend of Johnny Dedd, you stay that way until you die of natural causes or he decides to kill you. He doesn't have many friends. He appreciates those few he has. Joan was still a friend. I just hope she didn't 'friend zone' me. I feel like she is still madly in love with me, and I don't blame her. I'm charming... smart... well dressed.

Johnny lit a cigarette, which distracted me from my internal dialogue. He took a long drag and blew a cloud of smoke towards the floor.

Wait, he's smoking in a hospital...isn't that a bad thing? He doesn't seem to care.

He snorted a closed-mouth smoky nostril-sigh

before speaking. "I think Joan stepped in some serious shit. We'll need to talk to her."

I had to agree with him. There weren't many pieces on the game board for us yet. "I know... but I don't think 'talking to Joan 'is going to happen for a while. Do we even *have* a move right now?"

Johnny came up with a suggestion that was pretty good, considering our options right now. "Let me wander down to where the cops are guarding the other guys. Maybe I can pick up something."

"They're *your* fan base. I'll wait here in case she wakes up."

"They love you too, Tucker. I'm just a more colorful personality. Stump can wait here."

We had certainly earned reputations during our police careers. Johnny and I were both celebrities of a sort with the hard-nosed street cops. His only problem was his felony conviction occasionally causing some awkward 'associating with a felon' issues for our brothers in blue.

I asked him about it, "Are you worried about being a convicted felon snooping around the cops and smoking cigarettes in a hospital?

"Ancient history, cousin. All that felony shit was expunged. I got a full pardon, and a gun license. It's complicated. I'll explain it to you sometime, but maybe later. It's top secret or some bullshit." He took another drag off his Lucky Strike and blew smoke in my direction before adding. "And as for the cigarette, I thought this was America."

Johnny was a like mystery, wrapped in C4, stuffed inside a whoopee cushion, always living in that gray area between lawful and criminal activity, yet still full of surprises. I had no doubt his claim of a pardon was true. There were rumors on the street that he pulled off some heavy-duty shit for some sort of federal agents or something. Who knows? It's Los Angeles, that wonderful place where dreams sometimes come true, but mostly don't.

We waited another hour or so before doing anything to make sure Joan was going to be okay... it was almost sunset again, the brief window of daylight we get this time of year was almost gone.

There was no change so we decided to excuse ourselves and get started on the case. I guess it's a case now... and it's our case,Tucker and Deddario, the detective cousins. That sounds like it should be something, a TV show or book maybe.

As Johnny walked down the hall to dig up fresh intelligence information, my confidence level in his social skills was high. Cops seemed to either have loved him or hated him. Some considered him a mythical hero for drawing his duty-weapon and blowing an unarmed child-molester's head clean off in an interview room. Every good, experienced cop has thought about doing the same thing at least once, but they don't because they aren't psychos. Most cops are parents or at least the big brother or sister to a sibling, so the natural instinct to eliminate evil was inside all of them, lying dormant but not acted upon. And most cops have a line they won't cross, cold blooded murder being one of those lines. Johnny was a good cop, and was probably considered to be an excellent cop by his peers and supervisors back then, but he simply had a low tolerance for pedophiles. He didn't mind crossing lines in the furtherance of justice. His extreme actions earned him a stretch in prison. So yeah, the old school street cops consider him a hero. But the candy-assed pencil-pushers who are taking over police administrations across the country despise Johnny.

Johnny travels an unusual road. He has a lot of unexplained income, a whole bunch of convict pals who love him despite his being an ex-cop, and a shit-ton of cop pals who love him even though he's an ex-convict. The latest rumors on the street have him mixed up with a mysterious federal agency and some recently deceased movie producer, but street rumors are usually worthless and should be regarded at the same level of accuracy as the grocery store tabloids writing about aliens, hybrid bat-people, and England's royal family.

Johnny can sometimes be a difficult person to like if you're not a woman. With Johnny and me, though, it's a bit different. Like I mentioned, he's about my only living relative. Well, his mom lives on the east coast. I haven't seen her in decades. We do share a common grandmother, but she lives in the Valley and is a little rough around the edges. Full disclosure. Grandma even scares the shit out of me, even though she's ninety-years-old. She drinks like a fish, chain smokes, and tools around town still in her old black Ford Taurus. She still packs a Colt 32 automatic everywhere she goes. Her name is Gina Barton... her neighbor's call her Ma Barton. They are afraid of her. I call her grandma. I'm afraid of her too. But granny, aunty, and Johnny, are I all I have left for family. We have a weird relationship. But it works.

They say you can pick your friends, but you can't pick your relatives. They are correct.

Maybe Johnny would find some cops downstairs who were fans of his work. First pass he could go it alone. I'd let him work his special Johnny Dedd magic charm before I gave it a try. In the meantime, I needed a cigarette too. I couldn't make myself light one in the hospital, like Johnny. I gave Stump the *'going for a smoke'* hand signal and he gave me a thumbs up.

I strolled outside and across the street to have my smoke. I glanced at my Submariner. Five o'clock and it was as dark as pitch already. There was an evening fog lingering over the city. Locals call it the marine layer, drifting between the buildings, spreading a damp chill down the street. Street lamps glowed yellow and distorted through the moist air.

I stood under the street light, my Burberry coat keeping out the cool evening air... my hat protecting my head.

It was my kind of night.

A Los Angeles night.

Chilly, dark, and damp.

Then I spotted them. It was the movement... it caught my peripheral vision... A heavily armed crew of professionals moving briskly down the street toward the ER entrance, organized like ants, quiet as mice, and weapons at the low ready. It was either an extraction team or a hit squad, depending on whether they wanted to free their wounded compatriots or permanently silence potential squealers. Any cops or hospital staff who might get in the way were dead meat.

I assumed Johnny was chatting with the cops in the hallway this crew would be entering, not expecting a hit team to breach the ER. They were in an indefensible kill box.

I felt the Colt Diamondback in my hand before I realized I tugged the vintage wheel-gun out of my belt holster. Once again, I find myself having that internal debate. Why do I keep this antique instead of using a high-capacity automatic? I guess I simply enjoy luxury items and a 1977 factory-nickel-plated Colt Diamondback with a two-and-a-half-inch barrel is definitely a luxury item, at least in my opinion. But I could also have purchased a luxury high-capacity nine-millimeter automatic. So, perhaps the issue is not so much luxury as sentiment. My mom left me this gun after she passed. She stole it off some biker she had been banging back in the old days.

That makes it special. I think they call it an

heirloom. Never appearing as stolen in any data-bases makes the weapon legal. I try to avoid being too sentimental about life, but this old six-shooter meant a lot to me.

None of that mattered much right now. I had five heavy-duty bad ass looking guys stacking up to enter the hospital, presumably with intent to engage in nefarious shit. I glanced at the luminous dial of my vintage Rolex. Well, what do you know? It was time to kick some ass, which is a thing I'm not supposed to be doing anymore.

Did I mention I have only one fully functional lung and an unnaturally strong aversion to getting shot?

I moved closer. It made sense to use some of my high-order negotiation skills I picked up from hanging out with our mouth marines on SWAT. They had a female negotiator I really liked, and she taught me a few things... she also taught me some negotiation stuff. Hostage negotiators use precise and tactical language to resolve pending conflict leveraging psychology, analytics, and a vast know-ledge of human behaviors. I decided to go with that.

"Hey fuckers!"

They stopped and turned.

I took a pot shot at the closest guy.

I heard somebody yelp like a snake bit puppy, so I might have hit him.

I believe I have now established my dominance over the pack. At this point in our confrontation,

I should be in charge now, according to the principles of nature, negotiation, and human interaction.

But we were in LA. The laws of the jungle override the laws of nature.

Unfortunately, instead of surrendering to my alpha dominance, the rest of them started shooting back at me with automatic weapons.

So, I hid like a scared little bitch.

Diving behind the closest vehicle, I attempted to get invisible behind the relative safety of a full-sized pickup truck tire and wheel. I reluctantly took off my hat since there was no clean place to sit it, but I have watched enough westerns to know you always take your hat off while hiding behind cover.

Johnny and the cops... wait, that sounds like a good name for a punk band, doesn't it... let me rephrase that... My cousin and the LAPD officers came screaming out the door like a pack of wild cave men chasing a wounded mastodon... or whatever cavemen chased. I don't really know. Probably mastodons... or substitute tigers... no, that's not what they're called... what are they? I mean saber-tooth tigers... they were all running like one of those two things was involved. Full disclosure, I know little about caveman days. I *do* know about getting shot at though, and because of that, my ability to concentrate turns to shit now under high stress conditions.

A massive gunfight broke out and I believe in

the ensuing excitement, the bad guys forgot all about good old Joe Tucker. Johnny didn't shoot, which was wise on his part. But he *did* sneak up on the one I shot, a turd who was also hiding behind a vehicle in the chaos, and beat his ass like a rented mule. A live prisoner might help clear up some of this case. I was pleased that Johnny didn't murder him. Johnny tends to murder an above average amount of people. Some call him a homicidal maniac. He prefers to be called a robust problem solver. I'm neutral on the subject.

The police officers were clearly well-trained and they seemed to be very comfortable with the whole gun-fighting thing. They kill guys all the time in LA, not because there are a lot of violent cops in our beloved City of Angels, but because we have a lot of violent bad guys doing violent bad guy shit here. They often need to be shot.

LAPD scored a big win in this little song and dance, and thanks to Johnny's snatch and grab of the guy I popped, we had one of the dirty bastards alive and in custody. But the officers were forced to kill the other assholes. Sometimes that's how things work out. I can't say I give a shit. I'm just glad no more cops got shot tonight.

I stayed hidden while I secured my gun back in the holster, tugged my jacket over it, put my hat back on, and yelled. "Unarmed citizen approaching."

I came out of cover with both my hands up.

Two officers and a sergeant pointed weapons

at me and initiated a tactical approach to take me down, but Johnny, who had just handed a prisoner over to them, had my back. "He's a retired cop. He's okay. He's one of us."

The sergeant yelled across the lot at me, "We'll need a witness statement. Please stay at the hospital until we talk to you." The other officers went back to clearing the rest of the parking lot. I don't think they realized I shot somebody, and I wasn't about to tell them.

I noticed that Stump had responded to the gunfire as well. He didn't kill anyone either... what an unusual evening.

I joined Johnny and Stump at the door and we walked back to Joan's room together.

"Like old times, Joe." Johnny said as we gathered ourselves outside the ICU.

"Except it ain't," I said glumly. I missed the excitement of being a cop, but that kind of work wasn't in the cards for me anymore. I'm a borderline invalid.

Johnny ignored my comment. He wasn't a deep thinker, anyway. The nuances of combat resided outside his mental framework.

Stump spoke, giving us his assessment of what just happened. "Making a move on the cops like that is ballsy. They had to have some inside information. I'd like to talk to one of them."

I was dubious. "Sure, like LAPD is going to let us question their prisoner."

Stump clarified. "Not *those* dipshits. Their boss.

I'd like to find the Chinaman who sent those dirt-bags."

Being a sensitive human being, I addressed his politically incorrect description of the bad guy boss. "They don't like to be called Chinaman, Mister Stump. And I believe these guys are Japanese, not Chinese."

Stump didn't seem to give a shit. "Same thing, asshole... And I don't give a shit what they like. They're making moves in LA. I have people who will be concerned about that news. I'll need a name. Get it for me."

"How?" I asked.

"You're a detective. Take your cousin down there and chat up the harness bulls. They'll be bored and will give you something."

"Nobody says 'harness bulls 'anymore, Mister Stump." I regretted it as soon as those words escaped from my lips.

"Are you criticizing my diction?"

I saw his fist draw back slightly.

"Not even close to that," I said perhaps more desperately than I intended.

Were we even speaking the same language?

Stump grumbled dismissively. "Fine, then get to work or I'll do it myself."

I didn't understand how him 'doing it himself' was a threat, but I decided to not find out why. I'm disabled, not stupid.

I sought my cousin's assistance. He had already been down there once already talking with the police. "Come on, John. Let's try talking to the cops again and see what we can find."

He ignored my request and asked a question. "Are you packing?"

"Perhaps." I shrugged non-committedly.

He knew I was deflecting his inquiry with a vagary, an old cop trick.

"Leave your piece with Mister Stump or Deb... we don't want to get dragged into the shooting investigation."

"Yeah, well... I had nothing to do with that," I muttered.

"You probably saved my life." he stated flatly.

"Why would I do a stupid thing like that?"

"Because I'm your favorite relative."

I corrected his misguided statement. "Well, you are *not* my favorite relative... To be blunt, you're on my shit list."

"Because of what happened on the Bistavalle case?"

"I was thrown down a flight of stairs in that disaster of a case you dragged me into."

"You fell down the stairs."

"After I was stabbed."

"The guy threw a chicken at you. It's not the same thing as getting stabbed."

"Chickens have sharp feet."

I'd forgotten about the Bistavalle case. He dropped that turd on me around the time I wrapped up the Dead Eddie case. I owed him for saving my life on that one, so I had to work the

Bistavalle deal with him. I hate admitting the real reason he wasn't my favorite relative was because I was pissed off that he once dated Joan, so I went along with his assumptions.

Johnny pressed, "Look, dumbass... I know you shot the guy, and you saved my life."

"I admit nothing."

He acted as though he already won this debate, which he didn't.

"Of course you don't, Joe... now give the heater to Mister Stump and let's go, mister private snoop."

I don't like being called a private snoop... but I reluctantly surrendered my weapon to Mister Stump, who stuffed it in his waistband under a roll of fat.

I'd have to remember to clean my faithful Colt later.

Stump grunted something about staying behind and comforting Miss Deluca, the thought of which completely creeped me out.

I can't let my mind wander like this.

Johnny and I found a few cops drinking coffee down in the hospital cafeteria. They were the typical young blue suits, not rookies anymore, but not veterans either. They were still cocky, full of piss and vinegar. but guys you could probably count on if the shit hit the fan.

The cafeteria wasn't crowded. There were a few people scattered around the place... most were employees of the hospital The joint held the stench though of formaldehyde, green beans, and pepperoni, like most hospital cafeterias. Johnny and I grabbed a couple of coffees. He tipped the kid at the register a hundred bucks. Typical Johnny Dedd move. Somehow he got kind of rich in the past six months. Again, not judging and not looking too close.

We took a table near the officers. I let Johnny break the ice. He's a people person. People make me uncomfortable unless they are women. I am more of just a ladies 'man.

Johnny spoke in the direction of the officers without putting any of them on the spot to reply. "Any of you guys remember the city cop in Ventura County who killed three guys in an Oxnard convenience store and beat one to death with a case of beer?"

The approach was casual enough and friendly enough that one of them bit.

The oldest of the cops, who still looked like he was about fifteen, answered. "Sure. They teach that at the academy. Sounds like bullshit though. I mean, what kind of guy kills somebody with a twelve pack."

"This guy!" Johnny pointed at me with a big used-car salesman's grin.

"No shit? That was you?" A star-struck rookie exclaimed, eyes wide with astonishment at the sight of a real life super-hero in the room... and by real life super-hero I mean me, all modesty aside.

I've been through this before. Humility is the key to success in these things. I've never really been comfortable with the *hero* thing anyway unless the fans were girls, but I thought I'd go with the flow. "Yeah... but it was a long time ago, and I paid a heavy price."

"No shit. So you really tagged the guy with a twelve-pack of Bud?"

"No, Natty light. He wasn't worth a twelve pack of the King of Beers."

That drew a few chuckles from the group.

"So why didn't you shoot him?" another officer asked.

"Out of ammo and no time to reload. Shit went down quick."

"You guys from the old wheel-gun days were something ..."

"We learned to load from loops, kid. That shit puts hair on your chest," Johnny added.

The youngest of the group felt the need to mention that he waxed his chest. One of his pals called him a pussy. I doubted that he had enough hair on his chest to merit waxing. He could probably wipe it off with a damp cloth.

The oldest of the group engaged with Johnny and me, "Well, good job, man. That was some bad-ass level shit."

I felt a bit 'pumped up 'after all the praise, but I knew I deserved it so, there was that. I nudged the conversation closer to our objective. "Thanks, brother... so, what are you guys all doing here?" I asked, trying to sound like I didn't know exactly what they were doing there.

The chest hair kid explained, "Guarding some mopes. Asian gang shot a couple of our cops. We took some of theirs into custody. They came back here to spring them, but we kicked their asses."

"Righteous," I said, giving the kid a high-five.

"Semper Cop," Johnny said with a little salute.

"Fucking A," the oldest of them added, trying to sound tough, which was fine because I think he *was* tough. They might be baby-faced but these LAPD guys are no one to fuck with.

Johnny dove deeper into our covert interrogation goal. "So who are these asshats and why did they try to take out cops?"

The most baby-faced officer of the group answered, "I heard one of our gang guys say Yakuza... but who knows... I doubt if half the gang members in LA know what gang they are actually part of. The pukes who just hit us here were just an expendable crew of losers. Someone above our pay grade knows why they hit the OC detectives and who they did it for. All I can tell you is that these dead fuckers won't be committing more crime."

Johnny affirmed the officer's comment. "Yeah, like that sheriff in Florida said, *evil can't get dead enough.*"

"Yeah, he's a stud. Wish he was our boss instead of these cop-hating pussies we have in charge now."

"What do you mean?" I asked.

"They screw over any effective unit with their woke bullshit. It's almost like they're on the other side. And the organized crime division has been investigated for bullshit and is mostly getting broken up. It's weird."

"Everything woke turns to shit." Johnny added.

"That's a fact," an officer said to nods of unity from his comrades.

My phone buzzed in my pocket. I answered it.

"Yeah?"

It was Stump.

"She's awake... Get your dumbass up here."

"Johnny! Let's go. Our girl is awake."

"Shit!"

We scrambled back upstairs. I noticed there were still no cops waiting to take her statement. None of this seemed right. Where were her guards? Where were the detectives who should be with her? Where was her boss? The threat was neutralized... pulling off security was out of policy.

Joan's eyelids rose no wider than a refrigerator door opens when a kid checks to see if the light really goes out. She was still loopy, but awake.

I caught a glimpse of those beautiful green eyes gazing across the bed, glowing with what I know is gratitude and appreciation, as she realized Johnny, Stump, and I were hovering over her with faces full of affection, care, and concern. It was a beautiful thing.

I lifted her head and helped Joan to a sip of water... she swallowed it, cleared her throat, and addressed us.

Her face, full of heavy-lidded drowsiness, instantly slipped into a frown. "Shit... I went to hell."

Her mom leaned over our scrum, soothing Joan's concerns about the status of her immortal soul, "You're not in hell. We are still in LA County, baby doll."

I whispered to Johnny, "Is that better or worse?"

He had to think about it for a second before answering. "Difficult to say, but at least it ain't Baltimore."

I couldn't argue with him.

Joan struggled to sit up a little and failed. She spoke, unable to lift her head off the pillow by herself. "It was a setup, Joe. My partner and I didn't like it, but the LAPD Deputy Chief who's over Organized Crime and Gangs pushed our squad into rolling on that shit... They have to have someone on the inside undermining the organized crime unit. One of our guys got whacked two weeks ago too. Some high level...they have to..." her voice drifted off mid-sentence. She fell back asleep.

An older looking lady doctor came in and whispered back and forth with Joan's mom. Stump, Dedd, and I filed into the hall to powwow.

Johnny started, "Corrupt cops, gangs, ambushes... it's a war on honest cops. Not good."

"I know, right? But if someone from the inside is intent on taking down LAPD, we got to do something."

"Ain't that the fed's job?" Johnny asked, although his face displayed commitment to us handling it ourselves.

Stump answered his question, "No. It's our job now. They tried to kill one of yours... you kill all of theirs. It's in the bible."

"Are you sure of that, mister theology?" I asked with a bit too much sarcasm for Mister Stump to digest well. I immediately realized I had dialed up too much sarcasm by the way Stump blasted my solar plexus with his elbow. After I could breathe again, I continued, "You shouldn't hit a person with a missing lung like that, Stump. You could have killed me."

"I wanted to kill you. I'm actually sad you didn't die."

It's problematic to argue with solid logic like that, so I changed the subject while I sucked air.

"Earlier you mentioned talking to the Asian gang's boss. I think that is the best course of action right now."

Stump looked at me as if I had just eaten a worm, "Of course it's the right course of action, that's why I told it to you, dumbass."

Johnny intervened and probably saved me from another elbow strike. "So we all agree. Let's talk to the guy I caught. See what he has... get a name."

"He's in police custody." I felt like that needed to be pointed out.

"So?" Johnny gave me a devious smile.

I knew exactly what he wanted to do.

We couldn't find any scrubs or lab coats big enough to fit Stump, so he stayed with Deb and Joan. Johnny and I looked passable as orderlies in our stolen doctor clothes. We found a BP cuff and some other medical-looking stuff, put it on a metal tray, and made our way to the surviving gang members' room.

An officer was standing guard at the door. Luckily, he wasn't one of the guys we talked to in the cafeteria.

I tried to act like I knew what I was doing. "Time for this guy's dose of menach-de-diet-all-zone and hourly anal exam." I explained as we brushed by him. I'm not sure that menach-de-diat-all-zone is a real medicine, but it sounded like it might be. But the mention of an anal exam caused the officer to take a few steps away from the door and turn his back. Nobody wants to watch anal exams, at least not this far from West Hollywood.

Our guy, a big muscular Asian cat who was covered in scary tattoos, was cuffed to a gurney with an IV jammed in his arm, dozing. Even unconscious he looked threatening.

Johnny carefully took the items off the metal tray and placed them on a table. Then he smacked the guy in the face with the tray like he was trying to launch this turd's melon into the parking lot.

I joined in the fun by ripping the IV out of our subject's arm and punching him in the gut with a solid left.

I probably should have stretched first. I think I

hurt my shoulder a little.

But we had his full attention.

"Name your boss." Johnny demanded.

Interestingly, he was fully prepared to cooperate.

"Okay, it's Ayuma. Yamada Mister Ayuma Yamada. But he's not the main guy. I never met the main guy. Please don't hurt me!"

"How in the hell did you ever get in a gang, pussy?" Johnny asked very politely before smacking him in the face again with the tray.

"Stop please... I'll answer your questions."

"Why did you hit the cops?"

"They were getting close to the Mayor and deputy police chief, that would lead them to high ranking elected officials calling the shots... we own them all..."

Johnny gave me a quizzical look. "Aren't these guys supposed to be a bit tougher to crack than this? I thought they were inscrutable."

"That's kind of a racist stereotype, Johnny," I responded, wondering how dinosaurs like him and Stump don't have advocacy groups full of crackpot liberals following them around bitching about their language twenty-four-seven. After all, this *is* Los Angeles.

The prisoner answered, "Not really, most of us *are* inscrutable."

"Why you dirty intolerant asshole," I countered before punching him in the nuts. I don't tolerate intolerance... much... well, sometimes I do, just not this time. I'll be very candid. I've been in Los Angeles County my whole life and I still don't know exactly when something is politically incorrect or not. It's like painting the side of a moving train... They always change the rules, so I just go after the low hanging fruit.

I noticed Johnny was writing the boss's name on his arm with a pen, an old school cop technique. That's what I call report writing.

I asked the prisoner if there was anything else we should know.

He answered in a fairly articulate way for a guy who had been shot, had his ass beat, and been nut punched. "Not really, that's about it. We're supposed to kill all the guys in the organized crime unit. They were about to bust some LA Harbor thing, human-trafficking, drugs, pay-offs to elected officials... the usual."

"Have you ever considered another line of work? You totally suck at this."

"Are you hiring?"

"We don't hire pussies, sorry."

"Well, I was thinking of getting into bookkeeping. I'm pretty good with math."

"Are you just a total racist or what?" I asked incredulously at our cooperating prisoner. I was kind of glad I shot the intolerant little prick.

Johnny gave me a funny look. "Since when do you get your titties in a wringer about shit like that?"

"Full disclosure, cousin... I'm not usually concerned with social justice issues. I'm normal. I like to earn money and leave everyone alone who leaves me alone. But I was dating a neo-post-patriarchy-feminist, whatever the hell that is, off and on for the past few months. I didn't know she was nuts when we started dating. I picked up a few bad habits. She was totally a bad influence. I think she was a communist too. But she was hot. Sorry."

"If she was hot, I get it... but from now on, stick with lady cops and nurses," he advised. "They might shoot you but they never vote democrat and they hate everybody equally."

"Wisdom, Cuz... point taken."

"But the crazy ones are the best in bed, right?" he added with the charming Johnny Dedd wink that mesmerizes females but has no effect on me. But when he's right, he's right.

"There *is* significant evidence to support that theory, Johnny... but the price of obtaining that knowledge is too high."

The prisoner spoke up interrupting our philosophical discussion, "Are you officers done? I think I need a bed pan."

Johnny picked up a stainless-steel pan from a shelf. "Like this?"

"Yeah."

Johnny answered, "Sorry, pal. We're not officers, we're assholes." Then he smacked the guy over the head with the metal bedpan, knocking him unconscious. He looked at me and flashed another big Johnny Dedd grin. "Let's go."

I knew we couldn't remain in the hospital much longer without getting arrested for one of the many felonies we committed this evening, so our activities here had to be cut short.

We dashed into Joan's room. She was awake again and more lucid this time. I gave her a quick report. "You were right... this was a hit on the organized crime task force and it came from within the city's leadership... I think they are taking orders from someone even higher up the food chain... some high-level government player.

Her jaw set and her eyes became clear and focused. "Dammit... I knew it. I'm a sitting duck here, Joe."

She wasn't wrong. "We need to get your ass out of here, Joan. Something's not right and I think you saw something they didn't want you to see or heard something they didn't want you to hear."

"Yeah, and I don't know what that something is."

Deb spoke to Stump in a loud whisper, "The doctor was going to release her tomorrow. He says she took a graze to the head with a possible concussion, a through-and-through in the abdomen that didn't hit any vitals, and a couple in the vest that bruised some ribs... She'll be okay."

Joan interrupted, "Mom, you know I can hear you, right? I'm sitting right here."

"Sorry, baby."

Now Deb lit a cigarette in the ICU.

I had to get a plan together. I started spit-balling ideas like I knew what I was doing. "Joan, we need to bail your ass out of this shit show and reconvene at my office."

Stump offered a good suggestion. "How about your place? The office is too small for all of us."

He was right. Joan would be more comfortable there too.

I changed up the plan. "Fine. We meet at my place. Deb, I'll help you get her to your car. You," I said pointing to Johnny, "run cover and meet us there. Mister Stump and I will check out this Ayuma Yamada guy."

We undid some IVs, found her clothes, stole as much medical shit as we could carry that looked like something she might need later, and scrounged a wheelchair. We were rolling.

CHAPTER 2

The hospital parking lot

Stump and I hopped a ride-share and picked up his new Lincoln Continental. From his place we drove to Hancock Park where according to the database I subscribe to as a licensed private investigator, Ayuma Yamada owned a home. We found the place within ten minutes. It was a sprawling 1920s mansion just off Wilshire on South Rosmore.

Stump parked across the street. He opened his trunk and retrieved a delivery man uniform shirt and a small box. He carefully folded his polyester leisure suit jacket and placed it carefully in the trunk, then put the uniform shirt on.

He took the box to the neighbor across the street and rang the bell while I watched from the car.

An older woman answered the door and had a brief conversation with Stump, during which she pointed a couple of times at the house across the street.

He returned to the car, opened the trunk, secured the uniform shirt and put his jacket back on before returning to the driver's seat.

"Definitely Yamada's house across the street. We'll let this place cool off and come back later... or have a colleague pay him a visit.

"Who?"

"Don't worry about it."

I hate it when he says that.

He glanced at the ancient Timex Marlin on his wrist, "We need to get back to the office and join the others.

Johnny called me while we were on the way home, reporting that Joan was rallying by the minute. I think getting out of bed and moving around was helping more than hurting. I'm one of those who believe that lying around is no way to heal... or maybe I'm the guy who was in the hospital for a year and still whines about it every day. My convictions about healing philosophy are probably sub-par. Either way, I was glad she was feeling better.

In ten minutes, Stump and I arrived at my place.

We got through the doorway and the others were there waiting for us. Johnny's sorry ass was parked in my favorite chair. Deb was on my black leather couch... She was holding the cat. Joan was on her feet leaning against the kitchen doorway drinking a can of Buttwhisker beer.

Deb addressed me like a human being for a change. "What an adorable little black cat you have, Tucker. I didn't see you as a 'cat person 'before. Maybe you aren't such an asshole as everyone says."

She smiled like that was a compliment.

Maybe it was. I didn't think so. But at least she seemed to be warming up to me. And why wouldn't she? I'm lovable.

I decided to be candid regarding my cat ownership situation. "It's not my cat. It belongs to the neighbor lady. I don't know why it's here." I directed my next comment to the feline trespasser. "Why are you here?"

The cat licked its butt in response.

Cats are still not my favorite animal.

Joan harrumphed, as though she was perturbed about the cat getting more attention than a wounded hero lady cop. "Tucker, you got anything like a glass of whiskey around this zoo? This beer is warm."

"I have whiskey... tequila... and more whiskey... also a bottle of gin."

"I'll have a whiskey neat," she replied.

Stump jumped in, "I'll have a whiskey on the rocks."

Johnny added, "tequila with a lime slice, please. On the rocks."

"What do I look like? A cocktail waitress?" I asked.

"I used to be a cocktail waitress," Deb interjected with gleeful pride.

"I never would have guessed, Miss Deluca," I lied politely.

"Oh, yeah..." she elaborated. I worked at numerous establishments."

"It shows," Stump said, adding what might have been a compliment or insult. I'm not sure.

She took it as a compliment. "Why thank you, Mister Stump. You are such a gentleman... Tucker, show me where the good stuff is and I'll get the drinks so you can focus on saving the day."

At least she was right. I *was* going to save the day, more or less. Because I still love Joan... there, I said it in my head. I'll just leave it there until the time is right when she admits she is still madly in love with me. Then I'll tell her out loud.

As I pointed to the booze stash, Joan spoke up with a question I didn't see coming, "Tucker, I need to call my fiancé. Can I use your phone?"

"Fiancé? What fiancé? If you have a fiancé, why did you call me?"

I felt my heart sink. *How could she have a fiancé? What kind of woman gets a fiancé when she already has a guy she dated five or six years ago and has only seen a few times in the past four years?*

"Mom did call you on my city phone but you didn't answer."

Shit, the unknown number.

"I saw a call I didn't recognize, but I thought it was probably those assholes trying to sell me an extended warranty on the Mustang. I didn't recognize your mom's number."

Joan muttered, "I hate those warranty guys." Then she continued the story, "When we couldn't find you, I told mom to try Johnny because I knew he would bring you and you would need another gun with you for this shit. I trust you to help me break this thing. You're a world class asshole Tucker, a royal pain in the ass, but you always get the job done. Johnny and Stump are just a bonus, the heavy hitters. We will need that muscle before this is over. I got to stop these assholes from taking down the LAPD and I can't do it with anyone from the force, and I can't do it alone. I need you."

"So what does this fiancé guy look like? Is he gay? Not judging... But I know he's definitely effeminate... I understand strong women sometimes go for effeminate men... I mean, I read magazines and stuff... not sure if that rule always holds true, but..."

She interrupted me. "Tucker, will you shut up with your lovesick jealous bullshit? You and I broke up ages ago. It's over... Although I do admit you have some attractive points."

"I know, thanks!" I said, humbly... hoping to state my case, persuading her to dump her sissy loser broke-ass bum and be with a real man like me.

Johnny injected himself into our moment, or what I think was a moment... except for that fiancé part. "Hey, I have a lot of attractive points too. Small world," he said, as he ran a comb through his thick black hair, acting like he was part of this conversation, although he absolutely wasn't. "Do you got a mirror, cuz?"

"In the bathroom." I pointed it out.

He hopped up and dashed into the bathroom to look at himself. The cat followed him. It probably wanted to look at itself too. They are both creatures of vanity.

I returned to presenting my persuasive case. "Joan, I thought we were making some amends here. When we were at the police station that last time... and we..."

She cut me off before I could elaborate on our interview room make-out session last year. "Tucker, that was my poor judgment, a very big lapse of judgment... A total one-off. It will never happen again. That is a fact."

"That's not necessarily a fact... I mean, nobody can tell the future."

"Fact!" she shouted into my face and then abruptly slumped into a chair; pain etched across her face.

I shouldn't have upset her... she was almost dead a couple of hours ago.

"Are you okay?" I asked.

"I'm fine," she groaned in what sounded a lot like agony. "I'm just a little weak. I can roll, though. We need to stay on this thing."

"What the hell *is* this thing?" Stump asked. "I still don't know what the hell is going on."

Deb came in with drinks, serving us like we were guests at an elite beachside resort, taking care of Joan first since she was wounded. I guess Deb really does have talent. I almost felt like I should tip her, but it was *my* booze she was giving to these slobs.

Joan took a sip of her cocktail and seemed to rally again, although still not looking well.

I took a sip of my drink before speaking... Whoa! Deb pours them stiff. I let the burn of warm whiskey slide down my very parched throat and then continued. "We know we have a crew, or perhaps several crews, willing to go all the way on taking down the LA County Organized Crime Task Force. We know they wouldn't do this unless they were desperate. Nobody kills an honest cop unless they are a total asshole, communist, or they are scared shitless." I turned my attention to Joan. "What do you know that is frightening the hell out of someone and who exactly is that someone?"

Joan took a long sip of her drink, staring at me over the top of the glass.

My neighbor's cat hopped up in her lap, made a couple of three-sixties, then fell asleep. Joan dropped her gaze and gently petted the cat as she spoke. "Your instincts are sharp as ever, Tucker. It's big, very big. We were pulled off a political corruption case and sent to Long Beach for some minor gang shit... it didn't make sense. We wanted to hit a state senator's house and nail him for money laundering and bribery but we got shut down."

"Money laundering isn't earth shaking."

"She handles pay-offs for state election officials and is a pipeline for dirty money from an even higher official in DC. She also gets a handsome salary from foreign governments. That lady is a real powerbroker in the state and is possibly the most corrupt politician California has... and that's saying a lot."

"People don't kill over political corruption."

"That's my point. Someone is protecting people like her, someone in Washington, someone who is in bed with an Asian criminal organization. Someone who won't hesitate to kill a squad of cops that might have evidence that could take them all down."

"So, are you going to tell us who? Or do we just keep guessing?"

"Yeah, I'd like to know what we're getting into."

"Does the Senate Majority leader ring a bell?"

"Holy shit, he's been in office for like sixty years!

"He practically owns San Francisco."

She gave us a long hard stare. "Yeah, he's untouchable... but *we* can still arrest him."

Johnny didn't like the sound of that. "Not that I'm splitting hairs here, but we're assholes, not cops."

I felt as though I needed to push back on the asshole label being used so liberally. "I think that's the second time tonight you mentioned that, Johnny. I'm not an asshole. I'm a disabled hero."

Johnny didn't buy it. "You killed a guy with a case of beer and now you're a private eye... I think that puts you in the asshole category."

In retrospect, I guess perhaps he's right. But in

my defense, some of the best cops have the asshole gene.

Cross-talk in the room broke out as everyone started speaking at once.

Johnny mused aloud, "I heard that Senator had an enemy spy for a driver for like ten years."

Deb agreed, "Yeah, I heard that too."

I got in what I thought was a pertinent question. "Doesn't the Secret Service protect that turd?"

Everyone ignored me.

Debbie answered a question nobody asked. "I never voted for that weasel."

Joan looked at her quizzically. "Mom, have you *ever* voted?"

Deb shrugged it off. "No, but I watch the news. That's the same thing."

"Shut up, you assholes," Stump barked. "I'm trying to think."

Everyone quieted down while Mister Stump pondered our situation. He started running it down by the numbers. "Okay... Joan, what evidence do you have and how do we get our hands on it?"

She pursed her lips, probably thinking about the ethical aspects of sharing police intelligence with a hood, a PI, a goon, and her mom. She made a choice... all in. "I have tapes. I have surveillance photos... but what we really need if we break this thing is hard evidence a jury can sink its teeth into. The lack of a piece of physical evidence always kneecaps these white collar crime prosecutions."

"What is that physical evidence?"

"According to the wiretaps, it's fifty-million dollars arriving in cash at his house tomorrow night."

"Delivery by?"

"A paramilitary security team... goon squad, I guess. Maybe even foreign. Our target is an equal opportunity sell-out. He's in bed with the Yakuza, the Triads, the cartels, perhaps even the mafia to for all I know... He used Yakuza muscle to take down my team. He's in bed with all of them."

Stump threw his hand up like a cop stopping traffic. "Whoa, whoa, whoa, little lady. Do you have *any* evidence of traditional organized crime involvement?

She considered her words before elaborating. "No... but they are part of the criminal under-world, and our Senator is a crooked politician."

Stump got an intense look on his face and went nose to nose with Joan. "Let me explain some-thing, missy, and I'll make this very clear. There is no traditional organized crime in America... as far as you know. Second, these foreign mobs are breaking the back of domestic organized labor. That is something that is quite annoying to some very close legitimate business associates of mine. And third, this mob, as you like to call it, is back in the hands of the old guys again thanks to a one-legged legend who will remain anonymous. So, if there *was* a mobster around LA, not saying there is, he would be a very reliable and trustworthy mobster. Not one of those pretty boys you used to see in the news."

Joan gulped… "Uh… Okay."

Johnny elbowed me and whispered, "He's right, you know. Everything is better since the old guys are back in charge."

"That's your territory, Johnny. I'm just a private-eye for hire."

"Not tonight.

Stump repeated a very fake but loud throat-clearing noise until he had everyone's complete attention again. "Here's what we do. We jump that bastard in the middle of the deal. Bust 'em all. Call the cops. Joe, who is a licensed good guy, hands the whole thing over to the US Attorney. Or Joan can make the arrests if she feels up to it. The rest of us fade into the woodwork.

"Joan said our US attorney in LA might be dirty. What makes you think he isn't on their payroll?" I asked.

"Because he's on our payroll, dipshit." Stump explained.

"Oh…" I said contritely. Asking *who* he meant by *our* didn't seem prudent at this point. Stump can get a little touchy about the topic of the mob.

Joan interrupted with a raised finger. "I thought you said there was no organized…"

Stump stopped her in her tracks with an atomic stink-eye.

It was her turn to say it. "Oh…"

"About the secret service?" I tried again.

Joan answered, glad to end her uncomfortable conversation with Mister Stump. "They'll be with his wife shopping in Beverly Hills. He sends them away when a payoff comes in. He'll only have his private security team there. And guess what... they're all provided free by the Yakuza."

I persisted with my concern. "I didn't think they could 'send away' the secret service." I included the finger quotes like that evil doctor guy in the movies.

This time everybody gave *me* the stink-eye, including Deb.

Joan explained, "The Senate Majority leader decides for them. Let's leave it at that."

"Fine. I just don't want to shoot it out with the good guys."

"Who said anything about shooting it out? What do you think this is, a Bronco Hammer book?"

"Commie spies, Yakuza, crooked politicians, security agents... what the hell do *you* think is going to happen?"

"Not if we play it cool." Stump said, in not a particularly reassuring way.

"When do we ever play it cool?"

"We're playing it cool this time," he said in a way that ended that line of discussion.

"You have a plan," I asked suspiciously.

"Not yet, but I have an idea. We'll need everybody we have."

"We'll need a lot more than that."

"Perhaps. If we do, I can get more help. But for now we need to keep this operation between just us."

I looked around the room. Everyone was inexplicably okay with this ridiculous idea. Even the stupid cat seemed to be focused on Stump's comments and was purring loudly as it sat on my coffee table.

Johnny noticed me looking at the cat.

"What's your cat's name, Joe?"

"It's not my cat. It's my neighbor's cat."

"Does it have a name?"

"I heard her call it Poe, which is a stupid name for a cat. I have no idea why you'd call a black cat, Poe."

Stump interrupted our side bar conversation with a question. "Where can we get a bunch of guns in the next three hours?"

I'm in hell.

Johnny popped his hand up and shook it like he was in the second grade.

Stump, channeling his inner second-grade teacher, actually called on him.

"Yes, Johnny?" Stump said sounding uncomfortably similar to *my* second grade teacher, good old Mrs. Waffleknockers... or something that sounded like that. I can't remember the exact pronunciation... she was German. Her upper body was stout.

Johnny answered. "Okay, I know a guy. He has a storage locker full of weapons. He's a little shady, though."

I muttered to myself, "An arms dealer who is shady? What's the world coming to?"

Stump gave me a dirty look.

I decided to shut up.

Joan winced. "I need to lie down."

She did look a little pale.

"Let me help you," I offered.

I hopped to my feet to assist her to my bedroom.

The others started to get up to help too but I deterred them. "I have this," I said confidently. "You all keep working on the plan. I'll sit with Joan a minute and be right back."

She put her arm around my neck as we crossed the living room, entered the hall, and then the bedroom. I had my arm around her waist. It felt good. I caught the fragrance of her hair as it brushed my cheek. Was she wearing the new Byredo Mojave Ghost Hair Perfume? Very nice. She always had good taste. We carried something similar in the department store I worked in years ago.

Joan looked down and groaned as she sat on the bed, "Shit, Tucker... you got a boner? You pervert!"

"It's a condition." I explained. "I have low blood sugar."

I pulled aside some of the covers and she stretched out, attempting to get comfortable.

"You are such an asshole, Tucker... Not a total asshole. But an asshole."

I've been getting that a lot lately...

CHAPTER 3

My bedroom

Joan obviously needed some solid rest. Moving her might not have been the best idea. I wasn't spying on her but I did look at her cell phone, which she left on the nightstand by the bed. I noticed that her cell phone had been ringing off the hook and she didn't take any of the calls.

Somebody is trying to find her… and probably us too.

I'm pretty sure we were either wanted, hunted, or had been punted.

I sat on the edge of the mattress and held her hand. "You've looked better, baby."

"Fuck you, Tucker." She said with a half-hearted grin. "I can't believe I called you."

"Who else are you going to call? Your fiancé?"

"He's an accountant. Very smart… and handsome. His parents own a vineyard in France."

"Your mom already told me you made that fiancé shit up just to hurt my feelings… which I deserved. I messed up."

"My mom told you?"

"No, I just threw that out there just now to see

if you really had a fiancé. It didn't ring true."

"You are an asshole, Tucker."

"And you don't have a fiancé, hot stuff, which makes me happy. My biggest regret is losing you. Like I said, I messed up."

"Is that an apology, Tucker?"

"If you say it is, then it is." I caught myself and stopped being a wise-ass. She caught me too, and gave me the 'you dirty bastard 'look. I quickly corrected course. "I *am* sorry. You were the best thing that ever happened to me. But I blew it. It's on me. I'll take my lumps."

I gave her my best puppy-dog-eyes and made an extra effort to appear very sincere. I *was* very sincere, but I lie so much in my job that I could probably go into politics and fit right in. Joan is well aware I have this super-power so there is no fooling her.

"Tucker, the Ayatollah will be selling Bibles door-to-door in Mississippi before I ever get mixed up romantically with the likes of you again. But I'll admit, what we shared wasn't all bad. The door might be closed, but let's just say that I'm not ready to dead-bolt the lock yet."

That was music to my ears. Even though Joan was shot, doped up a little, and in agonizing pain, she gave me some hope. Unless she's delirious and thinks I'm someone else, which is possible. But now I was more determined than ever to win her back. I was breaking this case for her, for sure.

Or was she manipulating me and my friends

just to help her blow this lid off this corruption case? Why do I always go dark? What kind of person suspects every kind word is a lie and every gesture of friendship is a trap? Perhaps ex-cops who have been shot in convenience stores are that kind of person? Or private eyes are that kind of person? Or all of Johnny Deddarios 'relatives? That would definitely qualify one to be that kind of person.

But how is any of this my fault?

I might not have a choice about how I process information. It might be in my DNA. I should be more like Johnny. He can kill a guy and then go make a sandwich. How does he do it? I don't know. Maybe if a guy needs killing, he kills him and if he's hungry, he makes a sandwich, and it's no more complicated than that. Unfortunately, my level of introspection on life events goes a little deeper.

And I was doing it again, lost in my thoughts, out of touch with time and place. I need to talk to the shrink about getting back on my meds. Or maybe I'd have a drink and work this case instead. My shrink won't see me anyway since I screwed a gun in his ear for accusing me of displaying symptoms of hyper-arousal. Then I found out it didn't mean what I thought it meant... you can imagine my embarrassment.

I could see Joan's eyes getting heavy. It was time to rejoin the others. I meandered out to the living room, stopping every few steps to look back at the woman of my dreams... well, some of my dreams. Most of them, really... I dream about women a lot. I am such a pathetic horn-dog.

In the living room, Stump was really getting into this case. He was standing now, lecturing Deb and Johnny like a professor of outer space stuff when Haley's comet goes by. I know there is a name for professors who talk about outer space, but I don't remember what it is right now. Probably Space Doctor.

Stump turned his attention to me. "You and Johnny will take his Cadillac, meet his friend, and load up on weapons."

"What? Why? Weapons? What?"

"We're going to need fire power in the event of a worst-case scenario. Always plan for the worst and you can manage whatever contingencies come up in a situation. Remember that kid."

"Right..." I responded with more than a little concern in my voice. I've never seen Stump like this before. But he is the smartest guy I know, so... I'm in for the ride. I don't want to be a commando or whatever. I just want to get the girl and go home... but I am already home and the girl is in my bedroom... maybe I should quit right now. My goals have been met.

Johnny spoke next, "Let's go, Cuz... what could go wrong?"

"Everything, Johnny. Everything can go wrong."

Outside, I opened the passenger door and got into Johnny's classic caddy. I'd been to the Midway Museum in San Diego so I knew how big an aircraft carrier was. His car had to be the highway version. What a boat. But it was roomy and comfortable, a throwback to the age of Detroit in its heyday. Big black cars exude class, power, and confidence. My mood became more upbeat with every mile. I could see people along the way checking out our ride and giving us a knowing nod of respect. Things are looking up.

We cruised out of Long Beach and headed towards Riverside, which seemed like a long way to go to pick up an arsenal. After all, LA is full of off-the-book gun stores. But this wasn't just a small endeavor we were about to take on, so if we had to go outside of the city and buy quantity, we had to go outside of town. Somewhere off the 91 Freeway, we pulled into a commercial yard. It might have been a junkyard, or maybe just a junky yard. There were perhaps seven concrete block structures standing in various states of disrepair on what appeared to be a two or three-acre dirt lot. I saw more razor wire spread around the perimeter of the lot than the typical maximum-security prison uses for housing terrorists. I saw a few big ugly dogs that had the disposition of a guy with swollen hemorrhoids during a Preparation-H shortage.

A big dude came strutting out of one of the block buildings, crossing the grounds like he just won a title belt on one of those wrestling shows Johnny was always watching. He was an intimidating man, tattoos, watch cap, old army fatigue jacket, long hair, guns, heavy steel-toed boots, cigar, and black leather gloves without fingers. I noticed he carried what looked like a ten-gauge, sawed-off, double-barrel shotgun. It was a nickel-plated piece carried in one of those wanted-dead-or-alive leg holsters that Steve McQueen used to rock. He sported a jagged ring that looked like it could slice an artery... I didn't see this going well. He didn't seem nice.

Johnny didn't share my concerns. He gingerly hopped out of the car and embraced Mister Scary who returned the abrazo enthusiastically... he didn't smile, but he didn't kill Johnny either. I would have let him smell my hand first before petting him.

Johnny gave him a warm greeting. "Biker Bill Trevor... long time, no see, brother. How are your babies?"

"Doing great, Johnny Dedd, you crazy bastard... you want to see them?"

If this guy had the ability to seem happy, which I don't suspect him of, he was at least not overtly hostile. Obviously he had history with my cousin.

Johnny continued chatting up scary guy like he met gun-running psychopaths every day, which he probably did. "Hell yeah, buddy..."

At this point in their reunion, things seemed friendly enough that I felt it might be safe for me to step out of the car.

Johnny glanced my way as Mister Scary gave me a dirty look and touched his sidearm with his scarred and tattooed fingers. Johnny didn't miss a beat, "This is my cousin, Joe. He's kind of a puss, but good people. He has a cat."

I can't believe he went there. "I don't have a stupid cat." I instantly regretted my objection. Arguing with him about it made me seem like even more of a puss.

I waved at Mister Scary like a guy who was kind of a puss would wave. I'm willing to stick with the script if it will keep me alive.

Mister Scary returned my wave with a cautious nod followed by a cold glare of suspicion and distrust. I don't think he likes cats. Then he turned his attention back to Johnny. I lit a cigarette.

I'll freely admit, since I got shot, I *am* kind of a puss. I don't take chances anymore unless there is a damned good reason to do so, or if a beautiful woman is involved... not necessarily beautiful, but at least very good looking... or marginally attractive.

I forced myself to refocus on our gun deal.

Mister Scary, or as Johnny calls him, Biker Bill, asked the next question. " What are you looking for this time, Johnny?"

"The usual. Four MP5s, a Barrett 50, four 12 guage Benelli semi-automatic shotguns, and a flame thrower... we have our own sidearms... oh yeah, and a belt-fed machine gun if you have a spare, also I'll need two-dozen P32s... I'm running low again. Oh, and five-thousand rounds of ammo. Here's a list for the ammo breakdown." He handed

Mister Scary a piece of paper with what looked like some of Mister Stump's pencil scribblings on it.

I felt my blood pressure rise. *What the hell was he preparing for? A flame thrower? A belt-fed machine gun? What did I miss when I was in the bedroom talking to Joan? I should have paid closer attention or asked a few more questions.*

I decided in the interests of future self-preservation I should now resolve my nagging concern over the six-round limit of my Diamondback, so I rallied some courage and posed a question to Biker Bill. "What do you have in the way of a high-capacity nine-millimeter handgun?"

"I have almost everything that exists. But for a guy who is kind of a puss, I'd recommend going with the easiest, a Glock 15."

"I was on SWAT at one time, pal... I'll take a Glock 17 and a dozen thirty-round stick magazines." I almost said Glock 21, the forty-five caliber beast being even manlier, but something about the 21's thirteen-round magazine capacity made me uncomfortable. Not that I'm superstition about the number thirteen, but I already have a black cat crossing my path about fifty times a day. Why take chances? Beside, four more rounds in the box might come in handy before this case is over.

I was awarded an almost-smile from Mister Scary for my response. Johnny just rolled his eyes. I thought it was a pretty bad-ass comeback. I don't care what Johnny thinks. I still haven't forgotten how he once dated my almost fiancé.

Mister Scary sniffed in the air like one of his rabid junkyard dogs trying to capture a trespasser's scent, and then answered me with a curt, "You got it." I guess that's how he processes new information.

"Shoulder holster too?" I asked.

"No problem. Canvas messenger bag for your mags?"

"Of course."

Finally we were on the same page, merchant and customer coming to terms.

I lit another cigarette and walked back towards the gate while Johnny and Scary loaded up the trunk of the caddy with illegal weapons, well, maybe not all illegal. But in California, there is a presumption of illegality in all matters involving firearms. It sucks here. If it weren't for the weather, I'd probably move... nah... I'll never move. Who am I kidding? I'll probably die here.

Johnny asked another question. "So, that special item... do you have it?"

"Right here." Biker Bill retrieved a large canvas satchel from the bed of one of his many broken down trucks.

Johnny glanced into the bag

"Detonators?"

"Check."

Scary took Johnny around the corner to show him something else. A moment later Johnny returned to the car. I didn't ask questions.

I finished my smoke, lit another, then helped

Johnny and Scary finish loading the inventory into the trunk of the caddy. I noticed Biker Bill's shotgun looked like it had bloodstains on the stocks. I decided not to inquire about it.

When we were done, I slammed the trunk shut and waited by the passenger door.

Johnny forked over a big brick of cash wrapped in clear plastic. It must have been about a trillion dollars... probably not a trillion, but a lot of money. I have no idea where the cash came from. It seemed like a lot of cash for what we purchased... or did we just rent it? There was enough firepower there to defend a Korea Town convenience store during riot season.

What all happened in my apartment when I was in the bedroom with Joan?

Our business with Biker Bill Trevor concluded, we got in the car and headed back to my place.

"Johnny, how do you know that guy?" I asked.

"We were in prison together for a while."

"Johnny, how does a convict get guns? He's a prohibited possessor. This is a federal offense. I think you just gutted the Patriot Act."

"What guns?"

When he's right, he's right.

"I see your point."

Johnny changed the subject. I don't think he intentionally changed the subject; he was just done talking about that shit. "Want to hit a drive through for some coffee?" he asked.

"There is nothing I have ever desired more." I

leaned the seat back, pushed my hat over my face, and pretended I was somewhere else. A cup of coffee and a cigarette might just be my last meal... which is fine with me. I mean for a meal, not a last meal. I don't want to die in a hail of gunfire for this case. I've already been down that road once. But I've had worse meals.

Joe Tucker's Apartment

The joint was abustle when Johnny and I walked in. Stump converted my kitchen into a war room. Not that it was big enough for that sort of thing. It is a very small kitchen with seating for two at the little bar by the window. But Stump had taped a big map of LA County, some poster boards with drawings, and lists of names and to-dos on the walls. He had a bunch of colored pencils and markers scattered about. I have no idea where he got all that stuff or how he created his masterpiece of intelligence gathering and I wasn't inclined to ask. I joined him in the kitchen while Cousin Johnny flopped out on the couch, picked up the remote, and found some professional wrestling on my TV, which is probably the best place for him to be when there is thinking to be done. The cat joined Johnny, stretching out and yawning like all this commotion was normal operating procedure before going paws up and falling asleep again.

Why do cats sleep so much? Are there no mice left? Did there used to be more mice? What else do cats do?

I had to refocus again. My mind drift problem

was getting worse, probably due to the company I keep, lack of sleep, and rigorous alcohol consumption.

"Invading Normandy, Mister Stump?" I asked as I joined him in the kitchen.

"No, wise ass… I'm doing what should be *your* job." He grunted, never turning to look at me.

"Sorry… how's Joan?"

"She's in the bedroom with her mother. They'll be out soon. Go watch wrestling with your cousin. I have to get this ready for briefing."

"Briefing? What?"

When do guys like us have briefings?

Mister Stump elaborated although I didn't ask him to. "Joan outlined some approaches we can take to busting this guy. None of them are good but it's what we got."

I could feel my forehead involuntarily crumpling up like the skin of a shar-pei hound. It does that when I hear something unbelievable. "We'll need an army to take down this guy and we'll probably end up getting hanged for treason," I complained.

Stump countered. "Not if we bring on a cop we can trust, and enough guns, and maybe one more guy."

"Wait a minute, we don't trust anybody, especially the cops. That's what you are always telling me."

I tried to say the *we don't trust cops* part in Stump's voice but I just sounded like a constipated guy with a sore throat. Besides, the mimicry went right over his head… or did it? I was entering a Twilight Zone moment. Not the effeminate vampire twilights, but the old school Rod Serling Twilight Zone, the real stuff.

Stump explained further. "Look, I got an ace up my sleeve kid. And we got an honest cop to save *and* the dignity and reputation of numerous loosely confederated local business people who feel these gangs are moving in on our legitimate business interests. America needs us. Or are you going to be a pussy about it?"

"No, sir."

When Stump is right, he's right… and he's always right.

I tried to be more respectful. Stump is my financial advisor and life coach. He's also a de facto partner in my detective agency, just kept off the books. Plus, he's the oldest person I routinely associate with and I was brought up to respect my elders or get the shit kicked out of me by my abusive mother, God rest her soul.

Stump continued, "Look, we need LAPD to save LAPD. We will do the dirty work, let them take all the credit…"

I interrupted, "Like the FBI?"

"Yeah, they take all the credit like the FBI does… then we disappear with a shit-ton of money."

"What money?"

"Don't worry about it."

I might have mentioned it before, but I still hate it when he says that.

I pushed back. "No, Stump, I *am* worried about it. I don't know what the fuck is going on!"

He stared at me hard before speaking. "Are you *sure* you want to know?"

"No... I'm not sure, but I feel like if I am going to get killed in the next twenty-four hours, I would like to know why, or how, or just about anything that might explain why I'm getting my ass killed."

"Well you heard Joan's thing, right?"

"Yeah." I'm pretty sure I was the one who told Stump about it, but no sense pointing that out at this time. I don't need another elbow to the gut.

"Now the professionals are involved."

"LAPD?"

"No... my associates."

"The mob?"

"Not the mob. There is no mob. I'm talking about concerned citizens of Italian descent who have significant investments in organized labor, politicians, and various services that are offered outside the traditional retail business world."

"So... we're fighting political corruption, foreign espionage, and international criminals to save the LAPD by using organized crime... I mean concerned citizens, plus an old goombah, my psychopath cousin, a shot-up cop, and an old lady who used to bartend?"

"Yeah... that, and an honest LAPD guy, and then maybe one more guy."

"Who? Who in the hell from the Los Angeles Police Department could we recruit to make this day worse?"

For the first time in my experience, Stump was hesitant in answering. "Uh… you know him."

"Who?"

"Detective Sergeant Quinn."

"That fucking booze stealing abusive little leprechaun? He hates us!"

"Mostly he hates you."

"He's always trying to arrest me."

"And?"

"I don't like getting arrested."

"Quit whining. He's coming to help."

"Shit."

To an outsider, it might have looked like I was pouting, but I wasn't.

Stump read my expression otherwise.

"Quit pouting, you puss."

"I'm not pouting. I'm thinking. I need to find my bullet proof vest."

"Why bother, you'll probably catch one in that fat melon of yours."

"My head isn't fat. I just have a larger than normal head, like movie stars have. If anything, I look like a movie star."

"Lassie, maybe," Stump said.

"Asshole."

Mister Stump farted in my general direction. I decided to shut up. His toxic gas debate tactic is always a sure argument winner.

Apparently, Detective Sergeant Quinn is in now.

I dug further into the plan. "Quinn and who is the other guy?

"Don't worry about it. I'm not sure the other guy is coming."

"Fine, so Quinn joins the team. Now where does that leave me?"

"You're in charge of everything but the thinking. I'll do the thinking. If things go wrong, you take the blame, and I'll leave town for a while. That's the plan so far.

"So... normal plan, then?"

"Yeah, normal plan."

It was time to concede. Sadly, this discussion went about as well as all of my discussions with Mister Stump. This is what to expect when you negotiate with a brutally dangerous old hood that everyone in town is scared shitless of.

I voiced my submission. "Fine, let's do this. Show me what you got."

We were interrupted by Joan's mom who popped out of nowhere. "Bert, dear... would you like me to freshen up your drink?"

Nobody calls Mister Stump by his first name... what the hell is going on?

Stump replied to her, "Thank you, Deb. That would be so nice." He handed her his crystal bucket for a refill.

Stump is never courteous. What the hell?

"You want anything, Tucker?" she asked as an

afterthought.

"Sure, I'd go for a cocktail. Whiskey and water on the rocks."

She reached in the refrigerator and retrieved a beer. I noticed when she bent over, she still had a remarkable bum for an older woman. Stump saw me staring and slapped the back of my head.

"Knock it off, perv," he whispered.

Deb handed me the beer. "Tucker, you need to keep your wits about you. If this goes south, you're taking the fall."

"That is not reassuring."

"That's your reality, horn-dog... beer is all you get."

I shrugged and took the beer. Beer is delicious.

Stump continued, "We have a dirtbag US Senator receiving a massive bribe from a criminal organization that is from outside the United States, perhaps an unholy alliance of Yakuza and the Triad. They share a mutual interest in LA Harbor so anything is possible. A bagman is delivering the bribe. This bagman will have at least twenty security people with him. His security people will be either foreign military or criminals and they won't be missed should something bad happen to them, like us happening to them for instance. We will take our team in, take them all down mid-transaction, and turn over everything to LAPD, à la Detective Sergeant Quinn and Detective Joan Vance. The media will be there to make sure this goes public and Quinn will keep us off the radar."

"Sounds great but where does this media come from?"

"I got a reporter in the trunk of my car."

I didn't buy it. "Ha... bullshit... when did you have time to snatch up a reporter?"

"I drove downtown, snagged a reporter, put him in the trunk... easy peasy."

"So now we are involved in a kidnapping?" I asked, with increasing concern.

"When it's a reporter, it isn't kidnapping. They don't count anymore."

"Oh... I hadn't heard about that..."

He didn't wait for me to finish challenging his statement. "Most of the cops and hoods know. Also, everybody else who isn't a stinking commie knows. Reporters are bio-degradable."

"I see... so how does this takedown work?"

"We follow them in, jump them... kill all their guys, we hand the evidence over to Quinn, let the reporter out of the trunk, and we leave."

"And..." I knew there was something else. There is always something else.

"And Quinn lets us keep half the bribe money and we're out of there."

"Quinn agreed to this?"

"No... but he will. You can't save LAPD without a budget."

"I don't see Quinn buying it. He's the straightest shooter of all the straight shooters... except for some excessive force and brutality stuff. But of course, that goes with the territory."

"Let me take care of Quinn."

"You can't kill him! He's not a bad guy."

"That's not what I meant. I mean I'll talk to Quinn. I'm not going to whack him."

"Fine... then as far as this bust goes, we don't get involved or identified, right?"

"That's the deal."

"Excellent plan... except for every single part of it."

"What would you do?"

"Call the District Attorney for Los Angeles."

"Our target financed her election. She's worse than he is."

"Call the FBI."

"Did you hear what you just said?"

"Sorry... call the US Marshals."

"They're good but they don't have jurisdiction."

"Shit."

"Right."

"Fine...we'll do it... but we can't just go in and kill everybody and expect this not to turn into another Eagle Rock."

A hush fell over the room. Then Stump spoke very softly. "Don't *ever* say those words," he warned, obviously shocked at my mentioning... uh, you know what.

I knew I went too far. "Sorry... we just can't have another bloodbath. Right?"

"Right. No bloodbath. We'll do this strictly by the book so that way we can all get killed.

Dummy!"

"Wait, what?"

I don't want to get killed.

"Go drink your beer and watch some wrestling. I got to finish this then we'll brief."

I assumed he was dismissing me. But I wasn't taking orders from this big tub of lard so I dismissed myself.

On the big flat panel television, Gorgon the Immortal had some lesser brute, who I'm guessing weighs a svelte two-seventy-five, in a headlock while the crowd went wild. I identified with that 'skinny 'guy... the world had me in a headlock and everyone but me knows what's going on.

Twenty minutes and two matches later there was a knock at the door. I rose to answer since no one else seemed to notice it.

I quick peeked out the window and saw a cocky little prick parked on the door stoop, puffed up like a bantam rooster preparing to crow. He had on his standard navy blue pants and blue sport coat that almost looked like a suit, but the blues were slightly different. Someone without high-end retail experience in fine clothing, like I have, might not notice. But I noticed. Also, his sporting a brown leather pants belt with black wing-tip shoes was appalling. The out-of-date pencil mustache added a dash of sinister to his haughty attitude. His demeanor, his every move and facial expression, exuded the air of self-importance you often see in an old man with correct change in his pocket settling with a cashier.

Quinn might be short in stature, but he is a cop's cop. Honest, hard-nosed, and ready to cuff anybody for any reason or for *no* reason at all. His style of police work involved a generous serving of '*up against the wall dirtbag*' with just a dash of constitutional law added to satisfy the discriminating taste of the DA.

I get along okay with Quinn when he isn't trying to book me for no reason, which has been a common occurrence in our previous encounters. Normally I'd tell that swaggering shrimp to get a warrant before I'd let him in. But Stump wanted him there. I decided to open up the hatch before my porch was swamped with his rolling river of smug and conceit.

"Quinn," I stated flatly as I saw him in.

Quinn roughly brushed by me as he crossed the threshold. He wasn't buying my attempt at civility. "Shut up, gumshoe. Where's Stump?"

I think maybe he's more of a garden gnome than a leprechaun... garden gnomes are dicks and so is Quinn.

"Kitchen." I said.

He noticed Johnny Dedd.

It's not good to notice Johnny Dedd.

It's better to pretend like you don't see him.

Quinn didn't get the memo.

Quinn lit into him. "Hey convict... who let your sorry ass out of prison?"

Johnny didn't even look up from the TV... a

1911 Colt 45 appeared in his hand out of nowhere pointed directly between Quinn's eyes. "I like you Quinn... don't spoil it by being a dick... now grab a beer and watch some wrestling with me until Stump is ready for us... We good?"

Quinn started to say the wrong thing... then he caught himself. Johnny would burn him to the ground without contemplation or hesitation and he knew it. "We're good, Dedd... I'll just get myself a beer."

Quinn is cocky. But I've never known him to be stupid.

He turned toward the kitchen, but before he could take a step, Deb shoved a beer in his hand. "Drink this and don't bother Bert while he's trying to concentrate."

"I wouldn't think of it," Quinn stuttered, caught off guard by our veteran cocktail waitress and hearing Mister Stump referred to with a first name.

A minute later, three of us were yelling at the TV together, cheering on Brutus Justice, the main event good guy of the evening as he pounded on a couple of long haired slobs I never heard of. But they looked like dirtbags, so obviously they had it coming.

About the time that Brutus came off the top rope with an atomic elbow drop, Deb came in and made an announcement.

"Mr. Quinn, Bert will see you now."

Quinn, who as a member of humanity, was

afraid of Stump, which was smart. He did as he was told and scampered into the kitchen, which is apparently Mister Stump's office now.

Ten minutes later my diminutive detective friend returned to the living room, his face paler than fresh snow on a white bed sheet wrapped in some other white shit and covered with even more random white shit... he was pretty pale and I can't think of any more white shit or I would continue. Whatever Stump said to him, must have been some powerful juju. I suppose when you learn that an entire chain of command in LAPD is corrupted to a point where they will sacrifice a squad of their finest detectives to cover for a high-ranking elected official, you develop a severe case of prison pallor. Especially if the betrayal involves foreign agents, foreign racketeers, and fifty-million dollar bribes.

Stump came in behind him.

"Gentlemen," Stump announced, ignoring the shell-shocked Quinn. "We have an agreement with LAPD. Now let's brief."

Dutifully, we rose and left my charming twenty-four-by-fourteen foot living room to meet in my small but efficient kitchen, I mean war room.

Deb had set out hors d'oeuvres, which they must have picked up while Johnny and I were on our shopping expedition. Little dishes of trail mix, cheese bites, carrots, celery, and slices of pepperoni were spread out around the room. Deb found a folding chair and a patio chair and arranged the seating in a classroom style. Joan came in last; appearing to have significantly recovered since the last time we talked. She had color back in her face and she moved in her normal cat-like manner, quiet and dangerous rather than shot up and near death. Nevertheless, I could tell she was still hurting. When two people, like Joan and me, love each other, it is like we share a soul, we intuitively know what the other thinks. We share the utmost respect and love for one another.

Joan sat gracefully in the chair beside me. I knew she wanted me near her during this critical moment.

She gazed into my eyes and said, "Why did I get stuck sitting next to your dumbass?"

Maybe I am reading a little too much into our current relationship.

It was crowded but surprisingly comfortable in the new briefing room. Everyone had a seat, a small plate of snacks, and a beverage. The cat was sitting attentively by Johnny's feet watching Stump. I never noticed it paying such close attention to anyone before but the cat and I had never previously attended any formal briefings together that I am aware of. Deb provided the fuzzy little loafer with a little whipped cream in a coffee cup, which it seemed to enjoy.

Stump cleared his throat before speaking. He had a spatula in his had serving as a pointer as he lectured. Although, where did it come from? I don't recall ever having a spatula.

"This," he said grandly as he pointed to a spot on the map, "Is the Senator's mansion, where the exchange is going down. For the record, the amount of the transaction is twenty-five million dollars cash being paid by a foreign organized crime syndicate."

Johnny interrupted. "Point of order... I thought I heard the number fifty-million mentioned."

Point of order? What is this, parliament?

Stump answered gruffly, "Fifty-million is a number none of you recall hearing before." He followed that statement with a frightening sneer that would knock a starving rat off a dead pigeon carcass.

In response to the sneer, everyone gave the 'ewww' face with chin dropped, lower teeth showing, and eyes wide. Clearly none of us cared to remember that number being mentioned before.

I calculated that Stump deducted his twenty-five million dollar handling charge from the transaction, and then I pushed... No, not pushed, I shoved the whole thing out of my memory bank.

Stump continued, "Sometime between six and ten tomorrow evening..." He looked at his watch and saw it was two-thirty in the morning and refined his timetable accordingly. "Between six and ten tonight, we can expect an eight-car procession, twenty heavily armed security operatives with the money and as many as ten security personnel at the estate. The Secret Service will be off-property during this window."

Quinn sought clarification, "So definitely no good guys?"

"It's definite. The Secret Service Detail will be with his wife in Beverly Hills. We have some of my associates watching them and they will delay their return to the mansion as necessary during our operation."

"Associates?" Quinn asked.

"Concerned citizens," Stump answered.

Quinn wobbled his head in combined okay and hell no. He was probably disgusted by our plan but busting a crooked senator who would have good cops killed to protect his corrupt ways trumps generic disgust with normal criminal behavior every time.

Joan stood up and joined Stump at the front of the briefing room... kitchen... by my kitchen table... whatever. She spoke next, "I have good information that the caravan will arrive and the money will be taken into the house in four metal suitcases. The bribe will happen inside."

Quinn didn't miss a trick. "So you got a snitch inside the bastard's house, don't you."

Joan gave him a look that might be called coy or might be called coquettish. "Anything is possible in America, Sarge."

He obviously took that as a yes. I took it as good news. Having someone on the inside is the best advantage you can ask for on an operation... by the way, I'm calling this an *operation* now. I think we crossed the *stupid idea* line a while back.

Joan elaborated, "We'll have eyes inside. There will be a remote camera placed in the room where the payoff is going down. That's all I can say. Our approach will be tactical. The mansion is set on a hillside. The lot is covered with landscaping features, fountains, and statuary so there are plenty of places to hide. This time of year it will be dark by five so we have that going for us."

I raised my hand.

"Yes, Tucker?"

"Why don't we just use the video to bag this clown?"

Stump interrupted. "A reporter and a cop are going to find him duct taped in a chair, surrounded by dead foreign criminals, a flash drive with video of the transaction, and a pile of cash. We need to drive a stake through this piece of shit's heart."

I pursued the need to sate my curiosity, "Do we know what this bribe is for?"

Joan answered, "Unrestricted access to LA Harbor for their container ships, unloading of drugs, sex slaves, counterfeit luxury items, and stolen property to be done by their own personnel... and perhaps military hardware and CBRN weapons."

Stump interrupted Joan to fine tune her answer, "Without the assistance of American organized dock labor."

Joan added one more, not to be outdone. "And completely by-passing customs."

"How in the hell can they do that?" Quinn

asked. He looked like he could puke.

"A big fat payoff to our Senator can make this happen. Then he trickles down some cash and favors to the local hacks. "

"What an asshole," Deb stated.

She might be a little quirky but never doubt Deb's patriotism.

Johnny spoke next, "Why would Japan do this? They are an ally, and they are touchy about nukes, right?"

"Not the nation of Japan, were talking about the Yakuza, working with Jihadists, Russian organized crime organizations, and drug cartels."

Johnny wasn't pleased. "And none of those assholes will be getting involved in this deal, right?"

Stump took the question, "Of course not. That would turn this operation into a massive war instead of a simple arrest."

I was wondering how foreign agents could cut a deal with a government official to smuggle WMDs into the US, and how that would be okay. Are our officials in Washington that corrupt? Duh... Never mind, stupid question.

Quinn wasn't satisfied yet. "What about the dirty cops, the dirty state and local political operatives? They walk?

I was surprised when Johnny took this question. He isn't usually a deep thinker.

"Quinn, for years we started at the bottom and worked our way up the food chain to get the kingpins of these kinds of assholes. All we ever got was about one-third of the way before our cases always crumbled. And do you know why I think they always crumbled? They crumble because our bosses were bought off, or were morally vacant self-serving traitors. So, cut off the head of the snake. We work our way *down* the food chain this time. And hope we kill them all before they completely destroy LAPD and the rest of the Southern California police agencies. How many times have you watched the Feds work a case for decades only to tell us they have a half-ass wire fraud conviction they could have filed two weeks into the investigation. Or the suspect dies of old age. I say Stump is right. To take them all... we take them from the top down."

I saw a few chins drop. No one had ever heard Johnny talk that much before. I was feeling something that I hadn't felt for a long time, something other than an instinct for self-preservation and horny. I wasn't sure what it was but I think it might be pride. I felt proud of my two-bit asshole cousin. I was proud to have been a cop. And there was one other thing. I no longer felt tolerant of assholes trying to take down our country a piece at a time. I guess that's patriotism. Johnny Dedd is no George Washington, but he might be a drunk, vain, womanizing, psychopath version of Paul Revere. And when you are in the deep shit and facing certain death, you don't necessarily need someone who leads with lofty principles. You need someone with fundamental principles and enough guts to kill anybody in their way. You need a man like Johnny, Stump, or Quinn, men who will get the job done. Or Joan... a fighter who got shot and is already back in the trenches while her wounds are still seeping, leading the way without hesitation... Or a woman like Deb, who makes excellent cocktails and keeps the neighbor's cat occupied so it leaves me alone.

To be candid, I really don't know what the hell I'm feeling but I feel a lot of it and it makes me want to kick some ass for America. I know you understand what I'm trying to say.

Stump wrapped up his lecture with a tactical operations plan that had one unique feature... there was another player on our side he hadn't identified.

It was a simple plan. Those are the best plans. Stump ran through it one more time.

Johnny and Stump would be on one side of the driveway. A partner and me would be on the other side completing the ambush on the arriving bad guys and waiting on a signal from Vance. I call her Vance now because when we are operational, that's what she gets called.

Quinn and Vance will be concealed by the back of the mansion so they won't be eye-witnesses to the wholesale slaughter of enemy goons, and outside we would have Deb and the cat in the car with the reporter in the trunk.

When Vance gets the word from her inside guy that the Senator and the money are in the same room, the ambushers take down the goons. Vance and Quinn assault the building from their position and make an arrest. Stump, Johnny, Moses, and I carry out half the loot, tiptoeing back to the car over the bodies of many dead criminals and haul ass out of there. Then Deb and the cat gets the reporter out of the trunk, gives him the video, and points him to the arrest scene where Vance and Quinn become heroes and our reporter gets a Pulitzer. Deb meets us at my place and we divide the proceeds and drink heavily.

Quinn took a deep breath. He exhaled slowly before making a statement. I think he learned that breathing technique at the mandatory anger management class the city forced him to attend... three times. "This is stupid enough to work," he surmised..."just possibly stupid enough to work."

I felt like that summed our situation up nicely, although I think the plan passed the *stupid enough to fail* test too.

Stump gave us an order, "Get some rest... everybody... we convene in six hours and take this maggot down."

CHAPTER 4

It's not every day that I have guests in my house. Sometimes Quinn drops by to arrest me, my neighbor's cat comes by every day, but normal visitors here are rare.

Stump, Quinn, and Johnny went home for showers and power naps. Joan was in my bed. Deb was sprawled out snoring on the couch with the stupid cat. My sorry ass was parked in my big brown leather recliner with my hat over my face and a beach towel for a blanket. It wasn't great but at least the cat lost interest in me and focused on Deb now. Deb's coffee-cup-full-of-whipped-cream-treat probably won over the little feline terrorist's heart.

In a way, I was pissed off that the cat deserted me so quickly. Not that it was my cat. It belonged to that lady downstairs... I think. Or it used to belong to her. I haven't actually laid eyes on her in a long time now that I think about it. Maybe I *do* have a stupid cat. That would suck.

By the time six hours had passed my body clock was completely disoriented and I needed coffee and a visit to the head... not in that particular order.

I looked around the room and felt a feint wave of embarrassment as I realized how glaringly obvious it was that I seldom had company. My old Rat Pack poster crookedly hanging above the couch was dated. But I like art. The faded rug that I bought at a garage sale a dozen or so years ago might appreciate getting its first visit from the carpet cleaning dude. My big black leather couch had seen better days, all the cushions were breaking down, and there was a tear in the upholstery from when I fell asleep on my key ring. I might need to up my game. No wonder I am between girlfriends.

I got up and took care of business. I splashed some cold water in my face in the bathroom sink, and then went about the process of making coffee in the kitchen. I had a big thermos in the cupboard that I could fill and then make another pot. This army runs on caffeine... every one of us guzzles coffee by the gallon. It's kind of a cop, gangster, bagman, patriot, murderer, cocktail waitress thing we have in common... the cat, not so much, although it does seem to enjoy a coffee and Baileys, hold the coffee, lately.

I grabbed the thermos and went about making the first batch of coffee.

I heard Joan stir... I lightly tapped at the door and whispered. "You okay?" I waited for her to invite me in so we could share a sweet moment or two of staring into each other's eyes and exchanging heartfelt words of affection. Poor girl was still so obviously into me.

She answered with a harsh, "Get away from the door you filthy pervert. I'm trying to sleep."

I knew what she really meant was, 'please give me another ten minutes to nap, darling.' At least that's how I interpreted it.

I returned to the kitchen, poured a cup of coffee, and took it out to Deb. She was still snoring, so I set it on the side table and let the aroma of strong dark coffee waft through the air as a gentle wake up call.

While the ladies rested, I returned to the kitchen and went about reviewing the plan. The downloaded aerial map seemed to show a large wall around the Senator's compound. Stump wanted us to breach the wall and use the element of surprise. I hate surprises. They rarely go well. And how do you 'breach' a concrete block wall without using explosive materials?

Our plan was to take two teams, sweep the bad guys, and capture the senator. On its face, it seemed simple. But in reality, I could not envision any way that it would work. Just too many bad guys were involved. We needed an equalizer. In SWAT, we would kill the power and go in with night vision and overwhelming force. In the Special Crimes and Apprehensions team, we would disrupt their intended pattern of activity and jump the targets on the street. In this case, we had no choice but to take down the house with what we had. Not ideal.

But planning was the least of our problems.

The government had been corrupted and a corrupt government can be a very vengeful entity. I wasn't confident any of our lives, let alone careers, would survive this unless things went perfectly. As an aspiring entrepreneur and big picture thinker, this would not be good for business.

I heard a loud yawn and the flicking sounds of a cigarette lighter coming from the living room. Deb was waking up.

"Thanks for the coffee, asshole," she yelled in her rough 'smokes like a chimney' voice.

"You're welcome, Miss Deluca." I always take the high road.

From the kitchen window facing the street, I saw Stump returning... no sign of Quinn or Johnny yet. Quinn could have a change of heart and blow the whole thing. I had twinges of apprehension again.

Nah. What could possibly go wrong?

Stump let himself in.

Deb literally leapt off the couch and hugged him. "Welcome home, Bert. So glad you are back."

This isn't Bert's home... it isn't even your home, Deb... what is this 'welcome home' bullshit? What in the name of a ruptured duck, does she see in him? Stump is disgusting.

He gave her a hug and a kiss that was quick but not quite quick enough for my sensibilities. I couldn't tell if it was a romantic kiss or a mandatory Los Angeles lip brush. It was certainly not the old 'air kiss both cheeks' thing that used to be the standard City of Angels greeting.

Stump looked me over for a full ten seconds like I was a dead ground hog on a country road in July. He gives me that look frequently. I don't know why.

"Do I smell coffee?" he asked.

"Yeah, I'll pour you a cup," I offered as I pulled a mug from the cabinet.

Deb dashed into the kitchen and snatched the cup from my hand as she injected herself into our conversation. "I'll get it for you, Bert. I know how you like it."

How in the hell would she know how he likes it? She only met him yesterday. And I have been sharing an office with him for years. Wait... am I jealous of her stealing Stump's attention away from me? Do I need his approval to fulfill my self-esteem?

I came to my senses and realized what she meant. "The whiskey is back in the cupboard from last night, Deb."

She gave me a leering smirk and slapped me on the ass as she bounded merrily into the kitchen. That act of sass made Stump snort.

Since when did he start becoming amused by sassiness?

I gave up and flopped back down in my chair while she prepared his cup of hot black jitter juice with a healthy dose of Jackie D.

I lit a cigarette and enjoyed a couple of puffs while I waited for Stump and Deb to finish futzing around in the kitchen.

Finally, he joined me and took a seat.

"So, we're really doing this thing?" I asked.

"Yeah, it's real. But we're going to need another gun." Stump replied after taking a sip from his cup and then he followed with a shout out to the kitchen, "Delicious, Deb. Thank you!"

"Who can we get? Who do we know stupid enough to jump in on a gig like this."

"I'm trying to find the G-Man..."

"A fed?" I was confused.

"No, Mister G... it's his street name. He's an Ex-LAPD guy. But he's not around right now.

"Who else do we know?"

"I got nothing. Maybe Johnny will have a guy."

We gave up on thinking and focused on coffee in silence while Deb busied herself preparing some kind of brunch for all of us. I guess they had groceries delivered when we were out on the gun run. I've lost control over my home. But I can't say it isn't nice to have some company besides this stupid cat.

A few minutes later, the bedroom door swung open and a fully dressed, armed, and capable Joan joined us. Apparently, someone brought her some clothes from home while I was gone. A lot of stuff happened while I was gone.

Joan was wearing black military style pants that had to be tailored to be so tight. I didn't recognize the designer but they appeared to be designer war pants, if that's a thing. Her loose fitting gray short-sleeved blouse suggested a military style as well. I wondered if it was a Bottega Veneta knock-off. It wore nice on her. Her automatic was clipped on her belt in a black leather cross draw holster, slightly concealed by her blouse... she looked dangerous and sexy.

I wanted to tell her she was smoking hot, but I filtered my response considering the circumstances. "You look great." I offered, hoping to not get yelled at again.

"Thanks, Tucker. I feel better. I might be operating at around seventy-five percent now. Where are the others?"

Stump responded, "On their way, they texted me just a minute ago. "

So, our group was about as ready as it was going to get to face certain death, imprisonment, or worse... whatever is worse than death and imprisonment... something bad. I don't know. My optimism on this deal is not high. And I had a sinking feeling that when the identity of our final team member was revealed, it would not be Batman... and we will need at least that dude and some of his 'roided up spandex pals for this operation to work.

I heard a car pull up. I did a peek out the window to see who the new arrival was. Johnny's car parked a door down. He seemed to be talking to someone who was in the passenger seat.

A man exited the passenger door. He was dressed like Johnny, black jeans, black leather blazer, and cowboy boots... it's like a uniform for those guys... Yeah, I knew him.

Shit.

It was Moses Coulter.

I thought he was dead.

I was once hired to help Coulter with security for that radio guy who ran for Governor, but that gig was about six or seven years ago at some public speaking event. The last I heard he was a contractor in Afghanistan. And by contractor, I mean paid assassin.

I was certain I read he was killed over there, yet there he is outside my house. I didn't know Johnny knew him, but the Los Angeles circle of elite violent psychopaths was really a small community, so it made sense.

Coulter somewhat resembled that famous 1960s football player and movie actor, good old number thirty-two. The nasty-looking scar across his face ruined the resemblance though. Moses was stocky, tough, and big... six-three and two-fifty big. They say he was an Army Ranger but I don't know if that is true.

Coulter's claim to fame was during a brief stint with the Orange County Sheriff's Office years ago, he was cruising in his patrol car in Santa Ana when he rolled up on a couple of clowns trying to carjack some old lady at a gas station. He did the standard 'put your hands up' shit, but what he didn't know at the time was that the carjackers had two more bad guys in a car across the parking lot working with them. Coulter got caught in a crossfire as four hard-core veteran gang-bangers unloaded on him.

He flopped onto the deck and shot the two carjackers in their feet. When they fell holding their ruined dogs, he shot each of them once in the head. Coulter's combat shooting skills were scary deadly. Then he did a tactical reload as he sprinted to the old lady, throwing his body between her and the bad guys. He took two to his Kevlar vest but returned fire killing them both, again with head shots, but this time on the fly while diving through the air to save the victim.

He was famous for a while. It was something we had in common, the famous cop syndrome, except I almost died and he walked away with just some bad bruises on his chest. Coulter wasn't comfortable with staying in uniform patrol while every gang member in the OC wanted to take their revenge and whack him. A couple of times they did try jumping him, but he didn't even bother shooting them. He simply beat the shit out of his attackers and took them to jail.

When we last talked during that gig we worked together, he mentioned his ass was hanging out a mile and the department was indifferent to his risks so he made a tough career call.

Moses quit and went into executive protection and high-order security operations. He made some good money, stayed off the radar, and handled some shit from time to time that required extreme measures, perhaps outside the law... okay, definitely outside the law, but in the overall scheme of things, he remained a good guy throughout his career.

Long story short, Moses Coulter was a mean motor scooter and no one to fuck with. But he was as reliable to his friends and employers as he was dangerous to his enemies. Just a swell guy, really.

I felt better already seeing him show up.

A moment later, the two men with guns entered the room. Most people would consider that bad news, but I was happy to see them.

"Joe Tucker, how long has it been?" Coulter asked as we shook hands.

"Too long, Moses. I heard you were killed in Afghanistan."

"That's true. I was killed... but I walked it off."

Stump joined us, "Good to see you again, kid."

"Always good to see you too, Mister Stump," Coulter said warmly, vigorously shaking Stump's hand like he was just introduced to the inventor of the bikini.

When did they ever meet?

Johnny put his hat next to mine on the antique wooden hat rack beside the door. "I tried to hire someone who wasn't an asshole, but they were out, so I picked up Coulter," he explained.

After all the male ball-busting was complete, we concluded introductions and gathered in the kitchen.

Stump ran down the operation for Moses. It was good for us all to go over it again, so it wasn't time wasted.

Moses had one comment. "We're all going to

get killed... if we're lucky. Otherwise, best case scenario is life in Gitmo getting water boarded and yelled at."

"And?" Stump asked.

"No different than most of my jobs. I'm in."

Stump was pleased with the answer. "Good. I ordered some steaks and beer that should be delivered in a few minutes from that Australian place. I'll do some detail review with Moses, the rest of you eat then we leave in two hours."

So, that was that... we had a green light to go operational.

I need a cigarette.

CHAPTER 5

Outside Joe's humble home

I needed some fresh air, at least what passes for fresh air in LA, so I sat outside on the stoop in front of my apartment. I fished in my left front pants pocket for my SWAT Zippo and torched a Lucky Strike. The cat wandered out to join me like it was suffering from separation anxiety, and then promptly put me in ignore-mode. It does that sometimes.

"Do you want a cigarette, Poe?" I asked the black feline intruder, using the name I sometimes overhear neighbors call it by.

It didn't answer. It sat and stared at me with its yellow unblinking eyes.

Was it trying to hypnotize me? Bastard!

I decided to inform the cat that it will be in charge here until we got back from this operation. I was afraid one of those idiots inside would want to take it with us, which would be an unreasonable use of force, in my opinion. Cats are dangerous.

Am I talking to a cat?

I felt the buzz of an incoming call deep in my right front pants pocket as my smart phone vibrated near my happy place. I let it ring a couple of times before answering... you got to take time to enjoy the little things.

I didn't recognize the number.

"Hello."

An obviously digitally disguised voice spoke. "Why did Detective Vance call your phone?"

"Who?"

Police Detective Skillset 101 - Always answer a question with a question.

The robot-like voice seemed to ignore my question. "We know this number was dialed by Detective Joan Vance shortly after a shooting incident. Where is she? Are you Joe Tucker?"

"Do you have a name or do I hang up right now," I countered

"It doesn't matter who we are. Where is Detective Joan Vance?" Whatever software they were using changed the voice again.

I disconnected and flipped the device to airplane mode. No sense letting them ping my phone for a location. I hated to bust up a perfectly good yet outdated smart phone... but it still might have some use.

"Wait here. " I gave the cat another direct order.

It didn't acknowledge me. It licked its right front leg three times. Is that an acknowledgement? I'm going to say it is an acknowledgement.

I turned the phone back on, walked to the corner and waited for the next bus... I hopped on board, intending to surreptitiously ditch the phone in the luggage area, which was usually stacked with backpacks and suitcases. I was able to slide it into someone's oversized messenger bag before turning around to exit again before the driver could close the door.

The fat bus driver looked like his 4XL uniform shirt was five sizes too small. He made Ralph Cramden look anorexic. The top three buttons on his shirt were undone but his collar was still too tight under the rolls of neck skin and blubber. He sort of knew me from past trips, but he's never liked me. He's a dick. He doesn't respect my God-given right to disregard rules.

"You, no smoking on the bus," he grunted.

"I'm not smoking, slim," I said as I blew a cloud of smoke in his direction.

I discovered that he didn't appreciate irony.

"That's a lit Marlboro hanging out of your mouth, asshole," he barked accusingly.

I got in the last word. "You're not my favorite bus driver... and it's a Lucky Strike, pussy!"

I bounced off before he could worm out of his seat and I fast walked home as the bus rolled to the next stop. The cat was still on the steps standing guard so I sat down with it again. I guess under pressure it will follow orders.

"That call was weird," I advised the feline wanker.

The cat looked at me like it thought the call was weird too.

I finished my cigarette, while I processed what

just happened, and then went inside with the cat to report the news to Stump and Johnny. The cat followed me in but then immediately started making cat sounds indicating it wanted back out. I don't know what each meow means, so I guess from its body language that the message was supposed to tell me that it wants out again. I ignored it. I've been down that road before with the stupid cat, in and out, then in again. It's not my cat anyway.

Everyone was gathered in the living room when I came back in.

"Stump, I just got an anonymous call looking for Joan Vance. They had my name."

"Who was it?" he asked.

"They didn't say. That's what anonymous means... I don't know who it was. And the caller used a voice-disguiser." I called it a voice disguiser because if I used words like modulator or amplitude algorithm, Stump would kick my ass for showing off. I probably pushed it too far with the anonymous crack.

Moses postulated, "That's your dirty cops. What did you do with the phone?"

"I stuffed it in some guy's bag on a city bus."

"Sweet," Johnny said, voicing his approval of my ninja skills and mastery of deception, which inexplicably caused me to experience a brief sensation of pride. Compliments from a woman-stealer usually don't affect me that much.

Joan added, "They are looking for me... if the

good guys were trying to help me, they wouldn't be playing games with the voice shit. That had to be whoever is helping the Deputy Chief who sent us to the harbor."

I asked, "What is the Deputy Chief's name again?" I added the word 'again' to my query since it subconsciously suggests the other party already disclosed that information. It's a Jedi mind-control neural linguistics thing.

She answered without hesitation, "Deputy Chief Eddison Gray. He's a puss."

I slipped into the bedroom and snatched my notebook computer. I have some pretty good address check software that I subscribe to for the PI business, same stuff I used to find Ayuma Yamada. I found a home in Brentwood listed in the name of the Eddison Gray family trust. That block was full of very upscale residences, even for a Deputy Chief's salary. It wasn't that far away.

While everyone discussed the ramifications of the call, Johnny slipped something into my pocket, whispering that it was a cold burner phone. It was nicer than the one I had so I got a free upgrade.

Stump addressed the phone call issue. "If they changed the voice with a modulator using amplitude algorithms, then they were high-level cops, feds, agents of a foreign government, or my guys... and I know it wasn't my guys."

What the Sam Hell? Where did he learn that crap? The old man was full of surprises tonight. I hate surprises. And who are these 'my guys' he's talking about?

A bunch of old mobsters sipping espresso in sweat pants and gold-embroidered house slippers have that level of tech?

Johnny asserted, "So they are looking for Joan, they have your name... they will be here any minute. We have to jet right now!"

No one could disagree with his logic.

Stump gave an order, "Load up in the cars. Rendezvous at the DiGiorgio Trucking Company offices off South Santa Fe and Sacramento... the bad guys will be rolling up in two to three hours."

As Stump spat out the street number, I recalled that I knew the place. It was a dump, located behind another dump, in an alley near a worse dump. Not the greatest place, but it was close and too scary for most people to snoop around, so if things went south there, nobody nice would be at risk.

"And we are definitely not the bad guys, right?" I had to ask.

"No, we aren't the bad guys. We're something else... something worse," Stump answered grimly.

Joan, Johnny, and Moses left in one car, Stump, Deb, and Poe the cat left in his Lincoln, presumably with the reporter still in the trunk. I had told the cat to stay at my place, but I was not shocked that it disobeyed orders and went on the case with us. Following orders is not high on the list of cat skills.

I hopped into my old Mustang convertible but I didn't go directly to the warehouse. I had a different agenda in mind

Brentwood

The street was dark and the houses were mostly set back from the sidewalks dashing any hope of seeing anything useful from the car.

I had heard all the 'cut off the head of the snake' crap we talked about at my place, but I wasn't buying it. If we had a corrupt deputy chief of police in Los Angeles, I really couldn't wait to take him down. Especially since he ordered a hit on Joan.We were probably going to get sent to prison or killed tonight at the senator's house, so why not indulge myself.... Then I thought about Johnny Dedd and how he smoked a pedophile just because it needed to be done. I'm not a dangerous man like my cousin. I don't get in fights if I can help it. I only have one fully functioning lung... some people might even call me a bit of a puss due to my extreme aversion to danger. But this was an exception. He sent Joan to what should have been certain death had she not possessed some superior tactical skills. I had a creepy feeling he was the asshole who made the mysterious call to my phone. I wanted to talk to him.

The Colt Diamondback revolver rode high on my belt. The Glock was still in the trunk with the rest of my kit. For some reason I couldn't force myself to make the transition to an automatic yet. I slipped my Sinatra dress hat on my head as I got out of the car. It was time. No more Tucker being a puss. I needed to be Tucker the bad ass again, the man who killed a guy with a twelve-pack.

I walked along the hedgerow that divided the property lines. The hedge was about twelve foot high and seemed impenetrably dense. Most of the high-end homes on this block were separated that way. Sneaking from the street to the house was easier than I thought it would be. All the walls and sculptured landscaping provided more than enough shadows, cover, and places to hide.

Within less than five minutes, I worked my way around to the back. I could see a broad porch on the west side of the residence against a wall of glass doors. Behind the glass doors, I could see a large group of people in a sprawling room. Normal people might call the space a living room, but rich people who live in mansions call it the ball-room. I quietly creeped up to the edge of windows and peeked in, while remaining in the shadows of the adjacent shrubs. There were about a dozen Asian men and a couple of women in the room, well dressed and groomed, but reeking of criminal charisma. I suspected they could be Yakuza crime lords. With them was the usual diverse group of political hacks. It was a who's who of local high-ranking government officials, both appointed and elected... the Mayor, our deputy chief of police in question, almost the entire city council, and the DA. I wasn't certain, but the one woman with them seemed to resemble the congresswoman who represents South Central. Oh fun... I just spotted the owner of our local paper. I was embarrassed for the poor criminals for having to be seen with these scum sucking thieves and traitors.

I found an ear bud in my pocket, pressed it against the window and started recording into my phone. The window acted as a sound amplifier as the high resolution camera captured the action. I couldn't stick my handsome face up to the glass to see who was saying what, but I *was* able to overhear the following tidbits.

Tidbit one - "You will make the changes and blame it all on local criminals... preferably continue framing the Japanese syndicate."

Tidbit two, a different voice - "And we are each guaranteed three million a year if we can dismantle the police investigation and provide you with full unfettered access to the LA Harbor?"

Tidbit three, the first voice - We'll expect you to run cover for us with the local media, law enforcement, and your helpful activist groups."

Tidbit four, the first voice - ""We want every detective in the organized crime unit dead."

Tidbit five, the first voice - "The first payment is being delivered to the Senator's home in two hours. We expect results for our money."

Shit... I had them all cold and on tape... or I guess they don't call it tape anymore. I had hard evidence of corruption stored in my phone. I didn't need to confront the chief. I had enough to destroy him in my pocket.

But if these guys wanted to frame the Yakuza, who were they? I can't discern Asian languages and accents. I think it's because there are so many Asian languages and dialects spoken here and often there is no sufficient context to determine the speaker's nationality, I tend to gloss over it most of the time. I can tell French because they sound like the horny skunk in the cartoons, and I know German because they sound pissed off, and I know Italian because I'm part Italian and my cousin thinks he is the brand ambassador for Italy. Russians all sound like Boris and Natasha. But Middle East and Asian languages lose me. Maybe they need more cartoon characters from there.

My rumination ended when I heard a new voice pose a shocking question. It was the Mayor's voice. I recognized it from television.

"So, we can expect China's military to provide us with security and keep the US Intelligence Community off our backs?"

The answer to that question was even more chilling.

"Of course. With our influence, we can even direct them against your political enemies if you wish."

That led to a group chuckle inside the house.

Foreign guy continued, "Covert Chinese special forces troops will make the cash drop and will handle all security from now on, just like we protect your home. Just remember to blame all of LA's crime problems on the Yakuza... that will give the police and media something to investigate."

I felt like I could puke.

The core of Southern California political elite was in this house selling out the country.... and now I knew we weren't going up against local Yakuza organized crime thugs tonight, we were facing the elite of the Chinese military.

It was time to rejoin my elite team, if you could call an ancient fat mobster, a psychopath ex-cop, a dangerous mercenary, a wounded but still hot task force operative, a leprechaun with a sergeant's badge, a former cocktail waitress turned cougar, a black cat, and me an elite team. I know that some people might not consider us an elite team. I think of myself as somewhat elite. The cat obviously believes it is elite. But together we were definitely... something... I'm not convinced that 'elite' is the word I'm looking for. Maybe a better term will come to me later. But elite or not, we were the assholes who were going to stop the bad guys tonight...a group of very pissed off Americans. So the commies and traitors were in some deep shit, they just didn't know it yet.

I had aspirations of croaking Gray when I first got here, but that dream would have to be put on hold. Now it was more important to get back to the staging area and warn the others about what we were facing. I didn't have time to risk getting killed here now. I had vital information to deliver.

The black starless sky started to spit a little rain. I made my way back through the maze of landscaping features and returned to my car. There was no indication that I had been spotted so

I hopped into my old Mustang and hauled ass to the rendezvous. Things were a whole new level of interesting now.

CHAPTER 6

The Rendezvous

I parked near Johnny's big Caddy and other cars, out of sight and behind the ancient structure. The old building might have been a real prom queen beauty seventy years ago, but now it looked like the prom queen after thirty hard years of chronic crack addiction, prostitution, and alcoholism. Let's just say it lost its original glow.

The entrance to the interior was through a heavy wooden and steel reinforced door on the South side of the structure that looked like it was sturdy enough to withstand a nuclear blast. They used to build them all like that. I entered and climbed an industrial looking steel staircase to the second level.

The walk upstairs left me a little breathless. Between the Brentwood sneak and peak, the drive, and hike upstairs I was almost done. This one lung thing sucks. My mind says go and my body says whoa. I am not looking forward to my condition twenty years from now, that is if I live through tonight's dog and pony show.

I knew the team would be relieved to see me

show up as I entered what used to be a conference room in the second floor loft area of the abandoned building. After all, I am pretty much the leader, and dare I say hero, of our group.

"Where have you been asshole?" Mister Stump inquired harshly without even glancing up. He was probably trying to mask his joy at my 'better late than never' arrival.

I ignored his question and announced my latest findings to the team at large, "Things just got worse, boys and girls."

"How could it get worser?" Johnny asked, murdering grammar as ruthlessly as he murdered that pedophile.

"We aren't facing the Yakuza, we are facing the Chinese military. Their version of Delta Force."

"What the hell are you talking about," Quinn asked.

"Where were you?" Joan added accusingly, as I was peppered with aggravated faces and questions.

"I ran by Deputy Chief Gray's house," I admitted.

"What the hell for?" she asked, this time looking somewhat pissed off, as if my going there was bad... I wasn't the one who started this whole thing... but for now I won't say that out loud.

Knowing the truth wouldn't make it any worse, so I confessed. "I was thinking about shooting him."

Johnny Dedd smiled. "Crude. But I like your

thinking."

"What happened," Stump asked, now seriously interested. I think he saw the value of my criminal homicide turned intelligence gathering mission.

"That asshole has half the communist party in his house... which is a very nice house by the way... it has to be worth at least ten million. Beautiful... with a big winding staircase and..."

Joan cut me off. "Nobody gives a shit about his house, Tucker. What happened there?"

"There was a meeting... watch."

They all huddled around me as I showed the video I had captured on my phone. I hadn't had time to watch it yet so some of it was new to me too. Most of the time while I was recording at Gray's I was hiding outside the window. I had my face concealed and just filmed blindly, or recorded, or whatever you call capturing video now.

There were a number of 'holy shits' and 'what the fucks' mumbled among us as the six minutes of video ran.

Moses was clearly the most visibly pissed off of our team members. He's a gun for hire, but his patriotism and love of country is unquestionable and strong. And he also has anger control issues, not judging. Moses went into rant mode. "These scumbags are selling out the entire United States starting with Cali. This isn't just an LAPD corruption problem. This is the Golden State being auctioned off to the highest bidders."

Quinn, appearing shocked to his PD blue core,

could only manage to mumble. "This can't be real. This can't be happening."

Joan disabused us of any lingering doubts, "This is consistent with the intelligence we gathered, except worse. We need to make this bust more than ever now. No matter what."

I am virtually certain she meant we were doing this, even if every last one of us was killed trying... which is about normal for the kind of shit we typically get involved in.

Stump was not happy, but for another reason. "No commie slime is taking over the docks in Los Angeles. I got to make a call."

He disappeared out the door with his phone in his hand. I heard his heavy footsteps angrily stomping down the hall like a Karen on her way to talk to the manager. He had the cat curled up like a football, sleeping in his left arm. I never really saw him as being an animal lover. Maybe he was going to eat it.

I asked Joan if this changes anything.

"It changes everything, Tucker. We might be outgunned. But there is no choice for me. These treacherous dirtbags got my number and are already trying to figure out where I am. There's time for the rest of you to bail though."

"Not likely," Quinn replied.

Dedd agreed, "I'm not going anywhere... I'm here to see this through."

The others nodded in agreement.

It still looked like this was going to happen.

"Fine, we hit it as planned."

We started issuing equipment out of four large duffle bags They must have brought up from the trunk... speaking of trunks...

I asked Stump, "Do you still have that reporter in the trunk, or did he die?"

"He's fine. I just took him a sandwich and bottled water."

"Cool... I almost forgot about him. He'll need a copy of the video."

"Good idea."

Johnny dug another untraceable burner phone out of one of our duffels. We air-dropped the video clip to it, keeping a copy on my phone, and Stump handed the copied evidence to Deb. "We need to make sure the dickhead reporter has this after we secure the target."

Deb said, "Not a problem, big boy." Then she took the burner phone and dropped it in her cleavage. It disappeared in there someplace. She has a nice rack. I suddenly noticed she was looking kind of hot for an older woman. Deb casually leaned against the file cabinet that the cat was sleeping on with her hip jutted out revealing a shapely bottom and a tiny .22 automatic in her hip pocket. She had a form fitting dark green silk blouse that accentuated her generous boobage, tight jeans, and a dark blue watch cap. This cougar was ready to strike. She seemed like a natural for this kind of thing. In another life, she might have been a pirate queen. Joan definitely won the gene pool lottery with this woman for a mother.

I went back to prepping for the mission.

I took an MP5 and a canvas bag of magazines from the gear bags. I also found the Glock and shoulder holster and slung that on. I jammed one seventeen round mag in my hip pocket and dumped the rest of the Glock mags in the bag with the MP5 mags. I also kept my Colt revolver handy in my belt holster with two speed loaders in a leather pouch.

Stump grabbed an 870 Remington pump shotgun. I'm not even sure that piece was part of what Johnny and I picked up earlier. Everyone else kitted out too, looking like commandos... Johnny stayed chill in his black leather blazer, but he had a bullet-resistant vest underneath it. Naturally, Stump just stuffed pistols in his belt, ammo in his pockets and remained business professional in his ugly green polyester suit. He didn't don a vest. I'm pretty sure he is already bulletproof.

Johnny had the flame thrower, Moses had the belt-fed machine gun, and the rest of us divvied the shotguns and sub-guns.

Something was missing. "Johnny, didn't we have a Barrett 50?"

"Do you know what a wild card is, Cousin?" he answered.

"Yeah."

"Then let's not ask any more questions."

I could live with that. But what kind of wild

card would Johnny Dedd play in a game like this? It was a bit unnerving.

"Time to go," Joan announced.

Johnny quoted one of America's greatest heroes, "Let's roll."

It always makes me feel proud of our country when I hear those words. I guess Mrs. Obama have must overlooked the sacrifice that a group of Americans made in the sky over Pennsylvania when she was proud the first time.

The team now had a full load out. We were ready. It was time to get into our cars and go to see the Senator.

This time I had a partner. I think they told Moses to ride with me so I didn't go off-plan again. It was unnecessary. When the chips are down, I can stick to the plan... more or less.

Moses is usually quiet, but for some reason he got chatty and initiated a conversation. "Do you know wearing tactical gear over a suit with a dress hat looks funny?"

"Clown funny or funny funny?"

"Odd funny. I mean I get it… You want to look nice if they kill you but… I think you should have put on some jeans and a sweatshirt… just saying."

I didn't have an answer to that.

As we continued driving through the evening drizzle to the Senator's estate, Moses asked me a personal question. "What's up with you and Joan?"

"You don't know?" I was surprised at his question. I thought everyone kept up on the details of my love life. It's a big deal really... at least to me.

He shrugged like a kid whose friends were keeping secrets from him, a little bit 'I don't care' and a little bit 'FU very much.' "Nope... Well, nobody said anything. I just noticed the way she acts."

"Did she say something about me?"

I might have appeared a bit too eager with my response.

Moses snickered. I think it was the first time I ever saw his face do something that resembled a smile. He's usually an intense kind of guy. "No, Tucker... It's none of my business. Forget I asked."

I decided to tell him anyway. "We were engaged... kind of engaged... I guess I never gave her a ring or told her about it. But then she gave me the boot for almost no reason, after she caught me in bed with another woman. It was like she thought that was *my* fault so... you know how women always take things the wrong way."

"So true." Moses nodded in agreement. I felt he had been there and done that... we have a lot in common.

"Anyway, I always hoped we'd get back together... but, I don't think it's in the cards. Too much water under the bridge."

"I hope it works out for you. But you know we're all probably getting killed tonight anyway, so... what the hell."

"Yep... I had a good run... no complaints. If it goes south, I'm at peace with it. I mean, all you guys will probably get killed. I won't."

He laughed, "Why not?"

"I haven't been killed yet. I don't see any reason why that would change."

"Good attitude, brother. But I'll definitely go to your funeral if you come to mine."

"Deal."

We wheeled into a convenience store to top of the gas tank and pick up around a hundred bucks worth of surveillance goodies including beer, coffee, chips, jerky, hard candy, and cookies.

Nobody wants to go into combat without snacks.

Ten minutes after pulling in, we were back on the street.

It was a half-hour drive to our target. Moses and I reviewed the plan during the last leg of the commute. Wait for the bad guys, kill everyone outside, kick the door, and catch the Senator in the act. Then, duct tape our elected official's sorry ass to a chair, get some pictures, and finally release the reporter from the trunk of Stump's Lincoln so he could tell the world that Quinn and Joan were the heroes of Los Angeles. We agreed. This plan was so perfect it in its simplicity that it was almost foolproof.

The drizzle kindly paused for us. Everyone arrived at their designated positions as we started the direct surveillance of the Senator's home, all waiting for the arrival of the bad guys and cash. Moses Coulter and I found a good spot to set up our ambush. We were about twenty yards apart behind a two-foot high and thirty-yard long concrete wall.

I couldn't see the others and didn't expect to. They are professionals and our assignments were clear.

So here is the thing about setting an ambush, as the poet Horace once said, 'who can hope to be safe? Who sufficiently cautious? Guard himself as he may, every moment is an ambush. 'I'm not sure what he meant by that. But those Roman Empire guys didn't last as long as they did by being stupid. My takeaway is that the last thing you want to do is get ambushed while setting an ambush... So, we would have to not only keep an eye on our targets but also keep an eye out for a double cross, counter-surveillance, and cops too. I only know all this Roman stuff because a documentary came on TV and I couldn't find the remote to turn it off. It turned out the cat was sleeping on it. But the point was well taken.

I felt good with the crew we had, but we were going up against some stiff competition. Fortunately, in battle the unpredictable American will crush the hive-minded communist every time unless said Americans are double crossed by their own kind. Then all bets are off.

Then there is the old, nuke 'em till they glow and shoot 'em in the dark theory of combat.

We didn't have a nuke but I just received a text message from Johnny that the fifty-pound satchel charge of C4 we got from Scary Biker Bill, that mysterious last bag from the gun buy, was now in place against the foundation of the mansion in case things go wrong. If they capture us or overrun us, which is possible, we have one last trick up our sleeve. So even if we lose, we will still win.

That self-immolation finale may sound harsh but in the suicide mission business, it's still considered a big win... also it's funny to see their faces when they realize you are going to blow the joint to smithereens.

Only Stump and Johnny knew about the bomb before they told me in confidence at the staging area. No sense worrying the others about a technicality. It was expensive, but Stump had calculated it as a legitimate expense in the cost analysis he did on the project. I might have mentioned before, he's good with numbers.

So now, we were playing the waiting game. Waiting to see if a bunch of dirtbags were going to sell out California... at least more than they usually sell out California.

Waiting is never fun. It gives you time to think... and I started thinking about what the hell I was doing here.

I think Mother Nature was wondering what the hell we were doing here too. She took it upon herself to bend us over with a little dose of miserable weather, just to let us know who was really in charge.

Yeah, the rain started up again... just a little... it was the cold SoCal rain that either comes down in torrents or in annoyance levels of light spray and eventually drains into the sea. This time it was annoyance rain... Not a light drizzle but enough to cause a few thousand fender-benders on our streets and make us miserable. We probably should have brought ponchos... and some sandwiches. I was hungry again. We already ate all our snacks.

I'm cold.

I want to go home.

But if I go home, everyone will call me a puss.

Dammit.

We could hear them roll up... a line of black SUVs... I wish just once they would go with a different color or with big sedans, but it's always black SUVs. It would be cooler if they rolled up in a fleet of yellow hummers... that would be neat.

Moses gave me a nudge, shaking me from my car reverie... sometimes my mind goes off track.

Moses grunted, "Tucker, they're here."

It was time. "Get ready with the M-249, Coulter... There seems to be a shitload of dissatisfied customers arriving."

"Copy that." He double checked the squad automatic weapon, or as we call it, the SAW.

I think we both slipped into military mode. There is something about setting up an ambush with a belt-fed machine gun that brings out the martial stirrings in a man's heart. It's our happy place.

"Remember, let the main guys get in the house before we light up their security guys outside."

"Duh... what are you, my mother?"

"You're a mother."

"Blow it out your ass, Tucker."

Guys like us do our usual nerve calming bickering routine whenever an enormous amount of shit is about to hit a large ceiling fan... it worked.

Moses and I jammed plugs in our ears.

The noise generated by the SAW would be considerable.

I used my pocket monocular to monitor their movement. The vehicles lined up in the arching driveway. Men poured out of the vehicles and stood at the ready position around their respective cars. No long guns were visible but the men were certainly armed. A larger SUV, perhaps it was even a stretched rig, pulled up between the line of vehicles and the mansion. It parked directly in front of the main door of the sprawling estate home.

The scene seemed almost surreal. The beautiful polished brick drive glistened from the light rain. The landscape and security lights distorted colors and shapes leaving a near magical glow to what would soon be a killing ground.

An older Asian cat got out of the big car accompanied by five other Asian guys, two of whom were carrying large white cotton duffels... they looked like laundry bags... did we really need one more racist stereotype in this fiasco? What is this? Pick on Asians day? Sad. I was embarrassed that they would do that. But they had to be the ones delivering the big bribe.

The old guy seemed to be the boss. Through the monocular, I could see that he was a total dick and I hated him already. He had that arrogant sneer that super-villains have and walked like he owned the joint. I guess in a way, he did own it.

The six money men were dressed in dark suits, not uniforms, but close enough in style to confirm they were on the same team to any concerned observers.

At the moment when the bag bearing crew entered the mansion and closed the door, the final countdown would begin. Vance would send a text as soon as she had the word from her inside source that the deal was underway.

Six seconds later, her group text came through.

Hell was then released upon the land.

Four of us lit up the dirtbags standing around the SUVs. Stump was pumping rifled slugs into the crowd, Johnny was spraying with a sub-gun, and Moses let the light machine gun rip. I picked shots with my MP5, firing in semi-auto mode. Right now, I was wishing I had an M4 instead of this entry weapon but like they say, wish in one hand, and shit in the other.

Bad guys fell from our initial volley but not enough of them. They were good. I could see them diving for cover and making us work for it. Obviously they were not street muscle, these guys were soldiers... but not that elite. When I think of elite, I think of Seals and Delta... For China, elite just means they don't screw up their ops right off the bat and they believe all the commie crap. Political dogma injected into war fighting will weaken an army that way.

Elite or not, they were putting up a fight.

One of the things you run across from time-to-time that I am not a fan of, is return fire. It really sucks when they shoot back at you. I might have previously mentioned that due to traumatic experiences in my past, I prefer to avoid getting shot whenever possible. I'm not like Stump and Johnny. Those two go through life operating under the assumption that they can't be shot and if they are shot it won't be that bad. Oddly, that assumption has held true for them over the years.

The manicured grass in front of my cover position was suddenly chewed up by automatic rifle fire. I instinctively ducked.

The return fire we were now eating was level too... too much, too close, and too deadly. They seemed to focus on us as the SAW was wreaking the most havoc on their positions.

I spotted two guys breaking cover and moving to flank us. In spite of the chaos, I took my time and drew a sight picture on breaking bad guy number one. With a little adjustment to lead the fast moving target, I squeezed a round off.

Breaking bad guy one went down for the count

with his brains splattered all over the white stucco wall behind him. I think they will need a power washer to get that off and probably they'll end up having to repaint.

I tried to line up the second one the same way but he was fast. I had to rush my shot. He stumbled but made it to cover. It looked like I caught him in the upper right leg. That should piss him off.

Moses asked me to help him move the SAW. We gathered the weapon and ammo then moved to a better position with more cover and a superior angle.

"All yours big guy," I said before crawling down the slight slope closer to the driveway. I needed to get in tighter to their perimeter, find the guy I wounded, and then cut the rest of them off from getting to the house.

I found my spot near a statue of a kid who was peeing in a fountain, which I found disturbing on a number of levels. I always have. But I could see directly into their best cover, which was between the stretch vehicle and the line of parked cars. I went to work with three round bursts. They never saw it coming. A hint of panic appeared in their ranks.

And yeah, that's when I heard Johnny yell something from a movie about Nazi bastards as he came down his side of the driveway with the flamethrower. I can't remember what that movie was called. I saw it on the television. But it had the guy from some western or something in it, or there was something about a western in the movie... Full disclosure, I'm not good at remembering movies and I was a bit drunk and a bit busy with an attractive woman I met at the bar when I watched this one.

So, down he came from their position of cover towards the driveway. Stump was right beside him pumping and loading the old police style twelve gauge. The bad guys freaked. Most of them broke cover and ran towards our direction... unfortunately, they ran right into the SAW.

Moses lit them up like it was free. Dead villains dropped on the manicured lawn and brick driveway and for the first time in the fight, we were overrunning them.

I heard Moses yelling and cussing. He said something that sounded like 'murder every maggot they got,' which I thought was funny for some reason. He was really getting into it.

Johnny Dedd popped a guy who was trying to hide behind a car and jump him. He simply pulled his pistol and smoked the guy between the eyes without even looking. It looked like magic. My cousin might be a murdering blood-thirsty violent psychopath, but no one can say he ain't cool.

Stump stomped one guy to death, which was rude, but necessary, while he reloaded his shotgun.

To my right, I noticed Moses joining us, carrying the M249 like it was a toy, the last belt of ammo slung over his shoulder. Big men can pull that off.

"Did we win?" he asked.

"It looks like it," I declared, just a bit prematurely.

As I was getting ready to call Joan, something bad happened.

We had a certified 'oh shit' moment on our hands.

CHAPTER 7

While we stood in the driveway among the significant pile of dead guys we just made, additional bad guys showed up at the gate... a lot more.

Stump grunted, "This is unreasonable."

I believe he was correct. We already won our big gunfight and in a fair world, we should already be running into the house to seize the Senator and the money. Joan should be throwing herself in my arms kissing me in gratitude for all my heroic deeds. Our team should be exchanging high fives and butt slaps. But... that ain't what happened. Because life ain't all strippers and burritos. Sometimes life is an ice-cold shit-burger with no condiments and no fries.

Earlier I noticed a side gate on the property but didn't give it much thought. It didn't seem to be used much except for deliveries so it shouldn't have been a problem. Well, unless you consider ten carloads of assholes a delivery. Another ten came through the main gate, and they weren't random security goons. They were kitted-up paramilitary. We were flanked from two directions and there were probably still defenders in the house. I estimated we were facing four score and seven of them. Full disclosure, I don't know how many that is but if it is enough to worry Abraham Lincoln, it's enough to worry me.

Moses appeared dismayed. I heard him mumble, "That just ain't right."

A squad of four from the ranks of the bad guys started closing in as the others took positions of cover.

Johnny stepped up. My cousin is a natural badass... and he is not one to walk away from a fight. Fighting to the death is his happy place. In a clear and determined voice, Dedd asked one simple question loudly enough for all to hear. "Fight or die?"

His words created first a ripple, then a tsunami of warrior spirit in the group. I could see it in the faces of my team members. We knew, the bad guys knew, and probably whoever is watching over us from the heavens knew... we were going to die either way. So, we might as well go out as Americans.

For the first time in a long time, I felt like a real man again, a whole man. I was ready to meet my maker on my terms, going down fighting. I was ready to burn every round of ammunition, pull my knife, when that was buried deeply into the black heart of an enemy, then punch, bite, and claw at them until they killed every last one of us.

Then some asshole, who must have been on the roof during all this, dropped a couple of smoke grenades in front of the house and yelled, "Get the hell out of there!"

That seemed like a much better idea than all the macho bullshit that I had been thinking. So, we all ran like very fleet-footed sons of bitches around the side of the house and out through the backyard wall. Valor is great but it can be painful... and pain hurts. Fuck this last stand shit! I want to live!

I heard the report of the Barrett 50 being fired from the roof providing cover for us to make a break.

Joan and Quinn were still staged in the back of the house and watched in confusion as our fast moving herd of turds retreated for the woody hills behind them. They judiciously chose to follow us out.

We got to cover as a horde of evil scumbags, stinking of malicious intent, gave pursuit.

Johnny pointed to an outcropping of granite boulders, perhaps twenty yards across, probably stashed there for a future landscaping project. We made our way there and dove behind the rocks, which were now being peppered with small arms fire.

Moses Coulter caught my attention when he barked in his baritone voice, "What the hell?"

I looked. It was a resupply of ammo for the belt-fed machine gun stashed like we were expected. What the hell?

Never look a gift... some animal, I forget... tiger? Never look a gift animal in the mouth. That's a stupid saying now that I think about it. Animals don't have two things, opposable thumbs and money, so how are they supposed to buy, let alone wrap, a gift?

I helped Moses reload the SAW while everyone else found firing positions and slowed our pursuers with sustained cover fire.

The bad guys, and there must have been sixty or seventy of them this time, had been overconfident and rushed into the sprawling green lawn behind the house devoid of cover or concealment. Some mansions here in SoCal have large manicured lawns of a special low-cut tiff grass, like golf greens, that serves as a venue for outdoor events such as parties, receptions, and massacres. Not so much massacres before tonight, but... shit happens.

Our mystery roof benefactor stood at the peak of the highest point on the mansion. The full moon behind him, he appeared to me as an avenging angel of righteousness. I did three signs of the cross real fast. Johnny is usually the one doing that. He's the dedicated hard-core Italian Catholic, except for all those murders he commits. But Johnny was laughing.

Wild card?

The 1960s song by the Troggs started playing in my brain, except in a heavy metal version. Sometimes I heard weird shit in my brain. The man was definitely a wild thing to see.

"Is that a Roof Korean?" Quinn asked. wondering if the beloved patron saints of Los Angeles were the ones who just delivered us from certain death.

Johnny answered, "No, it's something else. A pal drove up from San Diego to lend a hand. You might call him a little dangerous."

Then an M60 machine gun the apparition was now holding belched fire as he unleashed hell on the scumbags below... not us, but the other scumbags.

I couldn't believe my eyes. A man with a face that could only be loved by blind mother... A man with forearms like a cartoon sailor wearing a black t-shirt and cargo shorts that revealed an artificial red, white, and blue prosthetic leg... A man with a butch haircut and a bunch of old school Sailor Jerry style tattoos, appeared on the rooftop like Santa Clause and dashed our despair away with a yellow belch of automatic weapon fire as he chopped our pursuers to pieces. The 7.62×51mm NATO cartridges tore through bad guys like a bag of drive-through Toxic Smell enchiladas going through Johnny Dedd's colon... which ain't pretty.

Now the tables had turned. I started thinking about Horace again... and that saying about ambushes. Which reminded me of that other saying by Roger's Rangers... Which I learned about in Cub Scouts... Because we had a cool Cub Scout leader... 'If somebody's trailing you, make a circle, come back onto your own tracks, and ambush the folks that aim to ambush you.'

Johnny and I were in the same Cub Scout pack,

but he must have paid closer attention to that lecture. Now we had our pursuers in a cross-fire... our life-expectancy had just increased by a factor of ten or more... whatever a factor is. I think it's a bunch.

Moses hopped up on one of the boulders in a single bound, like a big death grasshopper, or at least a big scary brute... or maybe a commando superman. He ripped loose with the SAW while Stump and Johnny advanced with long guns. Quinn and Vance joined them as we turned the tide and assumed control of the momentum in the fight.

It was a perfect kill box... Within four minutes, it was over. Bodies were draped across the yard draining blood and guts into the grass. At least the gruesome offal will make that grass green, which is nice. I guess we are environmentalists now.

"That was almost too easy," Johnny said, as he popped a fresh magazine into his MP5 and began the repetitive duty of popping head shots into the bodies to make sure they stayed dead. Johnny gets really focused on these projects. You have to respect that.

Stump lit a stinky cigar. He handed one to Moses Coulter too. I fired up a Lucky Strike. Sometimes that helps you stop your hands from shaking... not that mine were. Quinn and Vance were trying to decide whether to call this shit in to LAPD or start researching tickets to non-extradition countries. It was a smoke 'em if you got 'em moment in LA's long and storied colorful history of murder.

I asked the obvious question. "Who in the hell was that guy?"

Johnny did his usual deny everything routine, "What guy?" he answered as if someone asked him the time of day. He fired up a smoke, then gave me a look like 'you got anymore stupid questions.'

Stump was curious too. "Yeah, the roof guy... who in the hell was he?"

Joan had her hand flat over her eyes trying to see the roofline. "Where did he go?"

Quinn added, "Who was that masked man?"

Johnny asked, "What mask?"

Quinn didn't tolerate Johnny's bullshit. "Figure of speech, Dedd... I'm talking about that Kemo Sabe on the roof who just saved our asses."

Johnny elaborated, "He's nobody, just an old wharf rat from San Diego. I met him through that side job I scored after the whole movie director fiasco. He's a good guy. Karate teacher... "

"I don't see that dude teaching Tai Kwon Do at the mall, Johnny," Joan said.

"It's best we don't talk about him. He's gone and we won't see him again... if we're lucky... you know, he seems to be a shit magnet."

"Like we're not?" Moses asked.

"Never look a gift tiger in the mouth, people," I said with some authority as the informal leader of our team.

"A what?" Quinn asked.

"Gift tiger... it's an old saying. Read a book, you filthy leprechaun."

Quinn gave me the finger.

I grinned. My superior intellect and command of the English language and folklore won the day. Usually Quinn arrests me right after I win an argument, but he wasn't arresting anybody tonight. We all had too much shit hanging over all of us now.

Stump suggested, "Let's search the joint then get out of here. I hear sirens coming."

Johnny agreed. "Good idea. Mister Stump, you and Quinn search the house. I'll take everything I can find off of these guys."

I was a little uncomfortable with my crew making plans without running it by me first. It was almost as if they didn't acknowledge me being their boss on this operation. But it was a good idea, so... might as well roll with it. No point in saying anything.

Johnny took a canvas satchel from a body and dumped the pistol magazines out of it. Then he started robbing the dead guys. Maybe robbing is too strong of a word. He was collecting intelligence.... yeah... intelligence collecting would help the case. Maybe he'd find a map or a clue. Johnny was always a good detective, a real nose to the grindstone kind of guy.

I heard him shout, "Hey, this asshole has six hundred bucks and a gold Cartier Santos... I'll split the money with you guys, but I'm keeping this watch."

Johnny Dedd, always a man of integrity and focus. He'll always do the right thing when it comes to killing people who need killing, but he's a mercenary pirate at heart. The only reason he wasn't the black sheep in the family was because we were all black sheep.

"Has anyone checked on my mom?" Joan asked as she punched a finger at her cellphone like she was trying to get information out of it. She looked a little desperate. She was obviously spent from the injuries and battle. She plopped down on an area of grass that wasn't soaked in blood.

"I'll check on her," I offered. I was a little short of breath. But I tried to slow jog to where we left her parked on a side street.

I found Deb sitting on the trunk of the car, balancing the cat on her lap and holding a cigarette and a cocktail. Where did she get a drink in the middle of a gunfight?

"Deb, you okay?"

"I'm better than okay, Tucker." she cooed.

"What?" It seemed to me like she should be asking about the battle, the case, our mission, her kid... but no. She was chilling like she was perched on a cruise ship deck lounger.

"Some man, a real man, came running by with a huge gun, grabbed me, kissed me, and then just ran down the street like a beautiful jungle animal."

"What man?"

"Oh, he was sort of a salty bastard... tattoos, butch haircut, fake leg. He wasn't really pretty by any means, but man, can he ever kiss."

"What did he say?"

"Not much, just 'give me some sugar, baby.' Then he kissed me and took off in a big old Chrysler police car looking beast... what a man."

"That sounds like Ash."

"Who?

"Never mind, just some movie character."

"He was a character alright... wow!"

"What about the reporter?"

"He didn't get a kiss."

"I mean, is he still in the trunk?"

Deb put the cigarette in the corner of her mouth and slammed her fist down on the trunk twice.

I heard muffled swearing and thrashing coming from the trunk. I guess the reporter is still in there.

Deb asked, as she blew a smoke ring that lingered over her head like a halo, "All that shooting finally stopped, I take it you won?"

Deb doesn't seem to get rattled easy... Must be the cocktail waitress experience.

"Yeah... we won, but we lost... the bad guys got away and I think they took our evidence with them."

"Shit."

"Yeah."

The others came shuffling up carrying equipment and booty from the mansion, and gathered around the car.

Stump asked the obvious question. "What next."

"First things first… We need to get the hell out of here. Everybody meet back at my place. I got to run an errand first and I'll meet you there. Deb, will you drive for me? I'll need somebody to watch the reporter. He's coming with me."

"Sure Tucker… but…"

Stump cut her off, "What the hell are you going to do? That's *my* car."

"I'm going to get the evidence. I'll take care of your car, but I need to go alone."

"Alone? I thought I was going? What am I, chopped liver" Deb grumbled.

"I mean Deb and I."

The cat made an angry meow sound.

"I mean me, Deb, and the cat."

I heard something unintelligible that sounded like a muffled, '*watch a feck*' from the trunk. It's hard to understand people when they have a can- vas bag on their head and duct tape on their mouth. Or maybe he just has poor diction. Either way, he was going too.

"Me, Deb, Poe, and the reporter."

Stump growled a warning, "That Lincoln bet- ter come back in pristine condition, Tucker, or I will kick your ass."

"I'll take care of it… Don't worry."

Quinn asked, "Why would anyone name a cat Poe?"

"That's what everybody calls it… it's not my

cat. How should I know?"

Joan interrupted, "It doesn't matter what the cat's name is, we need to get out of here."

That comment seemed to break up the party mood, so we all hopped in cars and split the scene. Except I was on a mission. It was time to wrap this thing up.

Johnny gave himself a forehead smack, "Shit, I almost forgot." He pulled a little technical device out of his pocket and flipped the red switch on it.

Behind us the Senator's house and all the battle scene made a whoomp-kaboom sound and exploded like it was just nuked from space.

We drove away with a mountain of yellow flames in our rear-view mirrors.

Brentwood

Deb and I parked in the same spot on the street as my last visit to the Deputy Chief's house. I had probable cause, or maybe reasonable suspicion to believe... okay, I just hoped the cars that fled the Senator's house were heading here. With most of their guards dead, they would likely be desperate and return to a relatively safe location, the home of a deputy police chief. Thankfully the rain had let up. It was a beautiful night to die. The air had the fresh scent of the cleansing rain and it was just the right temperature to wear my Burberry over the bullet proof vest.

Poe hopped out of Deb's lap and stretched out on the dashboard.

"So, this is the place, Tucker?" Deb asked.

"Yeah, I'm going in for a closer look. If things turn to shit, head for the parking lot of that barbecue place on Brentwood Boulevard and Balfour... Go to the back of it and park among some cars. I'll find you."

"Got it.... and... good luck, Tucker... You're an asshole, but you always get the job done. And Joan is counting on you. We're all counting on you. "

That was the first time Deb ever really said anything nice to me, except for the asshole part wasn't so nice... but she said it in a nice way. I was moved. Maybe she would take the cat after all this was over. It seemed to like her.

I got back to business. "I'll need the reporter to cooperate."

She lifted an unusually cooperative Poe up off the dashboard and we got out of the car. I opened the trunk. The reporter was in remarkably good condition for being locked in a trunk for so long. I wondered if locking reporters in the trunk was a common occurrence and maybe he was just used to it. I sat him upright in a cross legged position in the trunk. I tugged the canvas bag off his head and shined the beam of my LED flashlight into his eyes so he wouldn't be able to see our faces. Then I ripped the duct tape off his mouth.

Don't ask me how often I am in a situation where I rip duct tape off someone's mouth but it happens often enough that I knew to flat palm his face when I did it so the yelping didn't draw unwanted attention.

I got straight to the point. "I need you to cover a story. It will make you the most important journalist in America."

He wasn't buying it. Screed to follow.

"Go to hell you bastard. I'm turning you into the cops and suing you into the stone age you kidnapping bastard."

It was like Deb and I were sharing a brain. I shoved him back down on his side in the trunk and Deb tossed Poe in with him as I slammed the trunk lid.

The first sound was a caterwaul of epic proportions.

Then came the shrieking. The reporter's screams were muffled but horrendous as Poe tore the reporter's ass up like it was unwinding a roll of toilet paper. .Maybe Poe and Deb and I shared a brain... only one of the brains was a cat brain that has a powerful fight or flight instinct, sharp claws, and razor teeth.

I could only imagine the war crimes level of bites and scratches occurring inside the trunk.

We gave it twenty seconds. I popped the trunk open and a now surprisingly docile Poe hopped out into Deb's arms. The cat looked sort of guilty, like it knew what it did, but it also looked like it didn't care. I'm not good at reading cat faces.

Speaking of faces, the reporter's kisser didn't look so hot this time. As a matter of fact, he looked like he just got a cutthroat razor shave from a barber with poor depth perception.

"Will you help us, please?" I again asked politely.

He didn't falter. He was smart enough to see how this was going to go down. "So, how do you want this story covered?" he replied, now totally on board with our mission.

"We're going to get evidence of corruption against a powerful national political figure and some high ranking local police officials."

He whined. "I would have helped with that kind of story even without the trunk and cat bullshit? What's the matter with you people?"

There's probably a whole lot the matter with us people.

I went into sales pitch mode. "Yeah, but think how much better the book you're going to write about this will sell with the kidnapping angle now. We really did you a favor."

"Oh… yeah… but I could have made that up. We make shit up all the time."

I looked at Deb. "He's pissing me off. Send Poe back in."

She held the cat at arms length pointed like a gun at our journalist. It hissed and showed its claws on cue, like a good kitty.

The reporter got suddenly religion. "No… the whole snatch and grab was a good idea, a great idea. I'm on your side. Thanks for kidnapping me and fucking me all up… Seriously. This really makes my career! You guys are great."

I'd heard enough blubbering so I cut him off and put the bag back on his head. "Fine. I'll get it set up at the house up the street. When it's time, my colleague will release you and send you to the scene for the story."

"Do you mean Deb?"

"Shit…"

"You know you used your real names, right? Stupid move, Tucker," the reporter snorted.

His attitude pissed me off, so I grabbed him by the collar and pulled his canvas-bagged head up close to my mouth so he would hear what I whispered.

"You like names, here's one. Are you familiar with a gentleman they call Johnny Dedd?"

The threat was effective. Tears and snot ran down his face as the sobbing ensued. "Oh shit… not *that* guy, he'll murder my family and burn my house down."

I think my point got across. But I slammed the trunk shut again for a few seconds to make sure he understood I was serious.

"Your words, not mine, newsie. We don't want our names mentioned. There are two cops who will blow the lid off this and I want them written up as heroes… got it?"

"No problem. I like living, pal… you got it.. .heroes, cops… .But no Dedd, right?

"No Dedd…unless you screw me over. Did I mention he hates reporters even more than I do?"

"Fine, deal… but please, No Dedd. We're good,

you'll get your story."

I had opened and closed the trunk so many times to talk to this guy I felt like Señor Wences... So I ended our conversation with a throaty z'alright. I was hoping he would answer with a z'alright, but I don't think this knob knew who Señor Wences was. Reporters are such pussies.

Deb knew Señor Wences. She held up the cat like a ventriloquist puppet and gave me a pretty decent 'z'alright.'

I closed the trunk lid and winked at Deb who gave me a wink back. We make a pretty good team.

"Do you still have that gun?" I asked her.

She slapped her right hip pocket and nodded.

"If this goes south, you might need it. Shoot everybody but me, if necessary. Then get the hell out of here and find Mister Stump. "

"Got it."

So now it was time. I was ready to continue with my heroic quest for justice and to do heroic things, as long as I didn't get too winded. My one lung situation sometimes holds me back when its time to do action hero stuff.

I checked my guns, the Colt and the Glock... ammo was topped off. I stared at the mansion down the street. It was time.

Deb slapped me on the ass and said, "Go get 'em, Tucker, you crazy bastard. Get the job done."

I blushed with pride at her comment as I walked to what would probably be my death.

CHAPTER 8

Stealth mode was the name of the game again. I could see people moving around in the ground floor of the massive house. I also spotted the cars that had escaped from the Senator's place parked back in the service driveway behind the guest house. Our crooked hacks and their commie pals were definitely here.

But would the evidence be there?

I found my hiding spot using the same approach and cover as I did earlier. I stuck my phone up to the window and started shooting some video, not so much for evidence as to see what was going on, who was there, what they were doing.

There was plenty going on.

At least ten guys were in the room that I could count. There could be more. I realized now that going lone wolf on this was kind of stupid. I should have at least brought Johnny with me... but that's a guaranteed bloodbath and if this goes wrong I don't want it to blow back on Joan... and not even on that evil pipsqueak Quinn either.

I monitored a little more... I needed to hear what was going down. I had my old hard-wired earphones with me. I put the microphone against the glass and stretched one earpiece to my right ear. I could make out what was being said and could capture some decent audio.

The conversation was curt. I think they were all pissed off.

The Senator was ripping everyone a new asshole. "I got dozens of dead assholes in my yard. How the fuck is that supposed to just go away? Seriously, How is that going to go away? I need you to fix this right now and I'm looking at you Deputy Chief Gray and you Mr. Ayuma Yamada... and you most of all Mister Dǒng..."

I started laughing when he said 'Mister Dǒng.' I know it's a common Chinese name but... dong is funny. And now I have confirmed that the Chinese and the Japanese were working together. Not good.

The Senator continued. "Look... there is fifty million dollars here on the line." He pointed to two cotton duffle bags in the middle of the room.

I'm guessing that's the cash we've been looking for.

"And now," the Senator said in an gradually increasing volume, "we have some kind of agents or something crawling up our collective asses. I want a team to go to my place and clean it up. I want a plane ready to take me to Tahoe, and I want my money."

Dǒng wasn't a pushover. "You might be in jail yourself soon. That makes you worthless to us."

A man I recognized as the Mayor of Los Angeles spoke up next. "Now gentleman. No need to panic. Nobody is going to jail, at least not from this group."

Then a woman's voice. "We're not all gentleman here, Mr. Mayor. Let's have a little respect for your betters."

I did a quick peek... Shit... it was a congresswoman.. She'd been a congresswoman since probably before most of us were born, the quintessential beltway parasite. I heard she banged Kennedy back in the day, which makes one wonder if he paid Oswald to shoot him after that hookup out of embarrassment... To encapsulate, she was evil incarnate.

So along with Gray, Dǒng, Yamada, the Mayor, the Senator, and the congress lady, there were four Chinese goons and three Japanese goons. I lost count of how many that was but it seemed like a lot... I think its thirteen. Not a great number. Not that I'm superstitious. I'm totally not superstitious. But still... why take chances?

Dǒng spoke next. I paid for a dead organized crime unit, control of a police department, a mayor, a congressman, and a Senator. I hoped my money would pay for that... but I have a very much alive organized crime unit, some kind of tactical force, and who knows else after me now. And you failed Senator."

Dǒng pulled a Sig automatic out of his belt and shot the Mayor in the face. I didn't see that coming. The congresswoman pissed herself, which was funny.

Dǒng waved the gun at the others, "I only shot this pathetic little man because he is the least useful to me. Seriously, he was pathetic."

The others, now gathering themselves nodded in agreement. Facts are facts. The mayor was a worthless little prick and it was no secret.

But I will allow that Dǒng now had everyone's undivided attention.

And then there were twelve.

I moved my position a little to get a better view. That's when I felt the cold gun barrel on my neck. It's not a great feeling.

"Get up. Get up, asshole."

Someone new… Now there is thirteen again.

It was a very large Asian dude who spoke perfect English, so I'm guessing he's an American like me, except sort of evil. After all, even though I'm hiding in the bushes at a house that belongs to some guy I don't know, I'm really the good guy here.

I got up as ordered, in spite of my status as the good guy.

He yanked the Glock out of the shoulder holster but he missed the Colt, which was on the five o'clock position on my belt. In the police department, we had a saying… always look for the next gun. This guy might be tough, but he wasn't a professional.

Considering the numbers,, I wish he had taken the Colt instead. But if six rounds was what I had left, it was better than nothing.

We walked around the house to the main entrance and entered. I hoped Deb was able to see me from down the street, if she was watching. She'd know what to do... or not.

Shit.

It was my first face-to-face with so many elite California politicians, a total bunch of dickheads. The Asian cats were a bit more intimidating. They were criminals but I had a sense that we had already killed off the first string and these guys might be the benchwarmers... you know what I mean by that, the kind of hood who gets assigned to steal bicycles and shakedown school kids for lunch money. They were young but seemed eager to prove themselves.

Not great. They're still dangerous.

"What do we have here?" The Senator demanded.

"Landscaper." I offered, hoping that his landscapers wore trench coats, suits, and a hat like Sinatra... really a timeless style, but not ideal for yard work.

I took a shot to the ribs. It hurt... I didn't even see where it came from... probably one of these kung fu looking shit-birds.

"Try again," Dǒng said.

"Fine... I'm a private investigator. Gray's wife asked me to try to catch him with another woman." I gave a shrug and a smile, "but that ain't likely is it... I think he prefers pumping chickens."

Gray reddened even more than usual, "I will

kill you for that, asshole!"

A couple of the Asian muscle guys couldn't help but snicker at my comment. But one of them didn't like it and I took another shot in the ribs.

"Okay fine... I'm a police officer. Internal affairs... but I'm willing to talk as long as you know it's the death penalty to kill a cop in California."

"Bullshit," a goon answered, "California hasn't had the death penalty for my whole life. They wouldn't even fry Charles Manson."

This turd might be the smartest guy they got. But I worked it a little longer, I had to buy some time. "Yeah, but Manson's dead, right?"

"How should I know?" Mister smart punk said defensively.

"He is."

"Cool."

Dǒng was upset about the conversation going off on a tangent. "Shut up... Who are you. I don't care about Charles Manson."

"Well, I'm not Charles Manson. He's dead."

Punch number three dropped me to my knees. It hurt too much to conceal the pain.

Dǒng approached me and grabbed me by the hair. "I don't really need to know who you are, I just need to know you're dead."

"No, that's my cousin."

"What?"

"Johnny Dedd. You hurt me and he will find you and kill you. Family pride."

There is an old saying in Los Angeles, timeliness is next to godliness. At least I think that's how it goes. And the timing was on my side.

As all eyes were on me, my eyes were at the back of the room where six large Italian men, bagmen, generic central casting goombahs, stood holding Thompson sub-machine guns. They were going old school with Chicago typewriters, also known as trench brooms, loaded with hundred-round drum magazines. Behind them in the shadows was Stump, Johnny, Coulter, and Deb.

I heard one of the bagmen say, "Hit the deck, gumshoe."

I hit the deck while the room lit up in flaming gun barrels. The firing paused long enough for all of Dǒng and Yamada's henchmen to finish dying. There wasn't much left of them.

The two head gangsters and the politicians were spared to this point. I scuttled over to my friends like a crab through a room full of twitching bodies.

Goombah one spoke next, addressing Yamada and Dǒng. "The boss wants a word with you." But the words sounded like 'da boss wunts a word wit ya.'

I don't see this going well for the bad guys... because they weren't dealing with good guys, they were dealing with worse guys.

"What boss?" Yamada asked.

"Da boss... you'll see. He's got some concerns about non-union labor at the docks."

I inserted myself in the conversation. It didn't

seem smart but there was something I wanted to do. "May I have a moment before you take them?"

The biggest goombah, not as big as Stump but pretty big, gave me a shrug and a weird head nod that seemed to say 'have at it.'

I walked over to Dŏng. He gave me a tough guy look. I didn't care for it so I gave him a stiff fist to the choppers. He went down hard. The guy had a split lip and enough blood on the ground to rewrite 'The Fixing Place' and another one. My hand hurt but it felt good. Then I turned and kicked Yamada in the nuts, just to be fair. I connected well and he collapsed and puked.

"All yours, gentlemen."

A bloodied up and wobbly Dŏng and Yamama were dragged out by the collars by three of the big torpedos. I had a feeling that the boss was going to meet them at the gravel pit or at a construction site where they would be pouring concrete foundations for a new office building. The other three big goons took the politicians and the Deputy Chief in tow and moved them to the library, which was a large open room full of books and shit adjacent to the room we were standing in.

I whispered to Stump. "I thought you mentioned some guys checking out Yamada's house from our recon... how did they end up here?"

"Yamada wasn't home so we burned down his house. Deb called Joan. Joan called me, and said she thought you fucked everything up and we should come and help. So, you owe us."

Somehow I felt that what really happened was Deb was concerned and called for assistance and because Stump loves me like a son, he rallied some troops and came to my rescue.

Deb added "Yeah, I figured they already killed you and we'd need to close this case ourselves. You shouldn't have hot-dogged it, Tucker." She put her arm around Stump, which means that she was getting sweet on the big mug and desired the company of a fat old bagman. That was the only reason she called.

I massaged my sore torso… "Swell."

"Joan and Quinn are on the way." Johnny announced.

I grumbled unenthusiastically, "Great." So far none of our plans had come close to going right, I was beat to shit, and everyone thinks I fucked this up.

Worst of all, I didn't finish what I set out to do. Close the books on a personal matter. I didn't square away the maggot who set Joan up to be killed.

I might not be a cop anymore, but if a corrupt cop sets up an honest cop, I consider myself to be back on the job, with unrestricted authorization for revenge. Because if a corrupt police executive will kill his own people, what will that scumbag do to the citizens of Los Angeles? Gray crossed a line. He set up Joan to be whacked. He got her partner killed. And he marked the organized crime task force for death.

When a police executive convinces themselves that their job is political, they tend to think in political ways and run with political people. They forget that the police department is a set-aside, a protector of all, above all the persuasion and agendas... they have a criminal code to enforce, people to protect, and equipment to do the job. Full stop. Anything beyond that, any other thinking, believing, justifying, leads down this road. It's a road to hell and a road to shame.

I thirsted for payback.

That's when Deputy Chief Gray, the dirtiest cop of them all, broke and ran. He obviously knew his own house better than we did, so he was able to dash down a hallway and out the back before we could stop him. I snatched a gun off one of the dead guys on the floor and chased the blubbery slug, making the best time I could after receiving the series of brutal punches and only having half my lung capacity. Dedd was busy with the politicians, slapping them around and introducing them to humility.

Luckily, Gray was a fat piece of shit and out of shape, so we were fairly equal in endurance, but if I catch him, he is still a hundred pounds bigger than me. But I have no intention of going toe-to-toe with him.

He disappeared. I stopped and listened. A lot of rookies will forget to hold their breath and listen in a foot pursuit. On a dark Los Angeles night, you won't always see them but you will always hear where they are.

The sound of someone sucking for air seemed to be coming from behind the guest house. I found him. He was leaning on one of the cars parked behind the guest house. He turned and looked at me.

"Who in the fuck are you?" He asked... his eyes afire with rage and panic.

I didn't answer. Instead I took a moment to survey the ground. Behind him was a sharply sloping hill leading to the next property, topped with an eight foot block wall. That was all I needed to know.

I pointed my stolen gun at him. I left my Colt in the holster. "That's it, asshole... you're done."

"Fuck you... I asked you once... who in the hell are you? Do you know who I am?"

"Yeah, I know who you are. You are the dirtbag who disgraced his badge and ordered the murder of an honest cop... a cop who is very special to me."

"Who, that bitch from the OC unit? Do you realize how much money is at stake? You could be rich. I can bring you in. You can have any woman you want. Let me go, go with me."

His words failed to endear him to me. I raised the gun and pointed it between his eyes. "L.A. doesn't deserve her... they might deserve your sorry ass. But not Joan... and you're not going anywhere but hell."

I felt a hand on my shoulder. It was Johnny.

"You don't want to do this cousin. Let me do it. No sense having this on your conscious... and I'll enjoy it."

Behind Johnny, I heard another voice. It was Joan. "Get a room, pussies." She stepped around us and stood between me and Gray. "Fuck you, Chief, you got my partner killed."

That was definitely concise and to the point observation on Joan's part.

Joan is what most people call a strong woman. A lot of women are referred to as strong, but they aren't strong like Joan. Joan is strong because she's honest. Joan is strong because she is ethical. Joan is strong because she is a dedicated public servant. She's also strong because, well, she's pretty strong. She works out at the gym every day. That's how she yanked the stolen gun out of my hand.

In a blink, she put one in Gray's belly, that hit with a splat and made his fat jiggle.

I think I heard Johnny snicker. I was kind of turned on... is that bad?

Her voice was cold as ice. "That's where the first bullet hit my partner you filthy bastard. He was a good kid. He deserved better than you."

She popped him again in the groin area. "That's for America, you traitor prick.

Gray screamed in agony. The pain from the last one had to be inestimable. I'm pretty sure she shot his business off. He made a sick yipping sound, quiet but pathetic... the rain started to drizzle again.

Joan didn't let up, "And this is for the good citizens of Los Angeles who we took an oath to protect and serve."

That round caught him in his open mouth and put him down. Very nicely done. Very nice indeed.

Johnny immediately went to clean-up mode. "I'll drag a dead guy out here and stage this up... everybody will be happy. I can see the headline. Hood kills corrupt deputy chief." Johnny took the murder weapon from Joan so it could be placed in the hands of one of the deceased gangsters.

"How are you going to explain a dead guy shooting a dead guy?" I asked, trying to clear up a hole in the frame.

"Hey, shit happens. He was executing Gray when one of the unknown assailants killed him. Forensics won't give a shit. They almost always just make the crime fit the narrative anyway. This kind of case for them is a dead gangster gravy train. They won't look close, they'll write short reports, and ship the bodies to the morgue, and move on to real people."

Joan and I put our arms around one another and had a moment. "

She whispered in my ear. Thanks, Tucker. You always get the job done."

"Yeah... it's what I do, baby. It's what I do."

We walked back in and caught the tail-end of the conversation between the remaining goombahs and the politicians. I heard something about someone getting whacked and some other explicit threats, so I think they came to an understanding. There might have been mention of a wood chipper.

I don't know for sure.

Stump took one duffel of money and left the other behind for evidence. Each politician got a knock out punch and were stretched out comfortably among the dead bad guys. It would make a great picture.

"Deb, bring in the reporter."

All of us went out the back while Deb and the cat ushered in the reporter and pulled the bag off his head and handed him a cell phone to take pictures with and then called 9-1-1.

While the reporter caught the story of a lifetime, which he could make up as he saw fit. I foresaw a headline that declared, rival gang wipes out crooked politician deal, or something like that in LA's future.

I think we made the reporter happy enough that he had a way to write us out of it. He had dirty politicians and cops with gangsters and twenty-five million dollars in cash. Nobody was going to be able to talk their way out of that. He gets a Pulitzer, the mob gets the docks back, and I get to play the hero.

The goombahs disappeared into the Los Angeles night. Quinn and Joan stayed behind to be declared crime-fighting heroes. Stump, Johnny, Moses, Deb, Poe, and I left for my place.

Another fun case more or less closed... it wasn't really a case, and it wasn't really closed, we simply killed everyone we could get away with killing, but the main thing is that it's over now and we could have a drink.

EPILOGUE

Johnny and I were the last ones to make it back, we stopped and picked up a bag of burgers at the drive through on the way which took forever. Don't get me started.

The booze was getting spread around and I saw Deb in the kitchen mixing cocktails in large batches with the cat. Moses said something about ordering pizzas. It looked like we were going to have a party.

Four hours later, everyone was passed out.

Twelve hours later Quinn and Joan arrived.

I was on the couch... I was afraid to think who was in my bed. Moses was in the recliner... Johnny was gone.

Our two now famous law and order cops went to the kitchen to make coffee as they tip-toed around our black-out drunk bodies.

I was sort of awake. I knew the others were there and shit was happening, but I was too hung-over to do anything about it. The cat was sleeping on my head. It does that sometimes. I think because twenty percent of your body heat goes out of the top of your head... I saw that tidbit on television. I gave Poe a soft shove and the cat pitter-pattered out to the kitchen to meow for food.

I sat up a little. The room seemed to move. Earthquake or alcohol poisoning? Probably alcohol. Joan came out of the kitchen with two cups of steaming black coffee that had that deep dark essence of coffee bean smell, one for her and one for me. She snuggled in beside me on the couch. Something was purring and it wasn't the cat.

"It looks like it worked," she said as she stroked my bed-head hair in place. "The politicos are in jail, internal affairs detectives are doing a round-up of scumbags at headquarters... Gray kept book on everybody involved. We found his notes. It was bad."

"Any blowback regarding the Senator's house?" I took a sip of the dark coffee... it was made the way I like it, black with two shots of Jack.

"Surprisingly no... It seems as if we weren't the only people who hated the Senator's guts. Everyone was more than willing to blame him for everything. I think I heard someone say, gas line explosion."

I frowned, "The senator might have my name or identification."

She smiled. "Good news. He had a massive cardiac incident on the way to the jail. He isn't telling anyone jack shit ever again."

"I hate to wish that on anyone, but I'll make an exception this time. I can't say I ever really warmed up to that asshole. How about the others?"

"They all lawyered up... but we got them cold.

I'm comfortable predicting an eight-by-seven foot room at the Colorado Super-Max in their future. Maybe they'll bed down with Noriega or whoever they keep in that hole."

"Yeah, he's dead. But they still got some other good ones in there."

"Yeah, so Tucker, about us…" her voice trailed off.

"It's okay, baby. I know you need to move on… I had false expectations, and I was an asshole to you. Consider me out of the way."

"No, that's not it. I don't want you out of the way. You're definitely an asshole, Tucker. But you get the job done. And maybe I have some feelings for you I'd like to explore. But I have to say, I never saw myself being interested in a man who has a cat."

"It's not my cat. It's my neighbor's cat, Joan. How many times do I have to explain that?" I was a bit miffed at the accusation that I'd have a cat. "Besides, Poe looks like he wants to be your mom's cat. They've been in combat together. That lends itself to bonding… I read a book on it."

"You didn't read a book, Tucker."

"I know."

Her pale blue eyes gazed into mine, mesmerizing me. I couldn't move. She leaned in and touched my lips with hers and brushed the softest kiss I've ever felt across my mouth, it was soft as a warm breeze, and to me it was a moment as beautiful as a Pacific sunset. I gently touched her hair and wished for the kiss last just a little longer.

For the first time in my memory, a wish I made came true.

After a moment I leaned back and took a deep breath, still locked into her softly smiling blue-gray eyes.

"Fine." I said. "I'll let you fall in love with me again, but just this one time."

"That works for me, Tucker. One more time is enough. I'll take it."

The end

Two Weeks Later - Joe Tucker Investigations Agency - Downtown Los Angeles

"So let me get this straight, Joan decided to retire and join the agency, Johnny wants to join the agency, Coulter wants to join the agency, and Deb wants to run the front office?"

"Yeah, that's what they're all saying, Mister Stump. It might be time to take it up a notch. Expand things. We still have Garza money coming in and the expense money from the Senator's house you gave us. I think with some new cases, it might work."

"What about the cat?" he said with much more sarcasm than necessary.

"Deb's landlord doesn't allow pets, so Poe is back at my place. But I don't think he wants to join the agency."

"The cat was the only one worth a shit."

"So, what do you think?"

"I think we're going to need a bigger office."

ABOUT THE AUTHOR

Bronco Hammer

Most days, Bronco Hammer invests his time writing hard-boiled extreme-action mystery and thriller books.

He is a retired law enforcement officer and has been a cowboy, treasure hunter, tech entrepreneur, wild fire hot shot crew member, and a bartender.

Visit Bronco's website at broncohammer.com

His wide range of interests including trucks, boats, motorcycles, cigars, whiskey, beer, muscle cars, horses, guns, sandwiches, and science.

He can often be found attending happy hour someplace on Coronado Island, California.

WHAT READERS
ARE SAYING

Scott Joseph - Donald Westlake step aside! There's a new King of Humorous Noir, and he'll drop the Hammer!

Dave Smith - Some authors have an ability to make you almost feel like you are there...but Bronco Hammer can give you a bloody nose!

Mike Ratke - A boot up the ass of corruption.

John M Sheffield - America! Hell yeah!!

John Laird - If you miss Mickey Spillane try a Bronco Hammer novel You won't be disappointed.

Chris Wells - The only thing better than a day of surfing is reading a new Bronco Hammer book!

Holli Lawton - Bronco Hammer never disappoints! When I started on this journey I was a mild-mannered granny. I've gone from meek and mild to bonafide bad-ass! And who says you can't teach an old dog new tricks? Thank you for your lessons, Doc!!

Skip Redpath - Bronco's "CAT" cannot put his books down... The CAT says they are purrrrfect!! (Author's note: I don't have a cat... it's my neighbor's cat, don't listen to what that old Leatherneck Redpath tries to tell you.)

Kenny Wilson - When the snake charmer is unleashed, evil flees, thus the true story of the Colt Python told by the Cold Steel author BH warms the long-legged models as they know a man is their companion.

William Tullock - Writes a story the way us LEO's would like to tell it without having to be PC.

Aahdree Gee - Bronco Hammer has given me a reason to get up in the morning. His books are totally relatable and remind me that I can be badass, hardcore, and sexy all at the same time. I can't wait for the next one so I can set even higher goals!! Thank you, Bronco for bringing out the best in me!

Earby Markham - Are you sensitive and cultured? Does gratuitous sex and senseless violence offend you? Are you upset by continuous macho posturing? Well sweet cheeks, Bronco Hammer books are NOT for you.

James McLaughlin - "I suggested Bronco's books to a friend. He told me "After reading two of them I was raging like a stallion."' Not exactly sure what he was referring to, but I'm sure it's something good. as are Bronco's books. Hai Karate!"

Freeman Rockdale - If a cop did his job, he either has PTSD or lives in a bottle, or both. When you read the Hammerverse, you begin to kick it all to the curb. Stand taller, straighter, and much calmer. And laugh. Laugh a whole lot.

Scott Long - To say it will blow you away, well, that's an understatement.

Steve Casillas - Shared similarities between Bronco Hammer Books and the Fraternal Order of the Eagles - Mothers Day is a priority and No communists will ever be welcome.